Was that a Diaper?

It was almost unmistakable in the moonlight flooding the warehouse, the waistband poking out just above the man's pants as he bent down to pick up a knife. *Great, not only am I caught, but I'm caught by a guy who isn't even potty trained,* he thought...

Chapter 1

"Boss, what're you doin? Don't'cha think this is a bit evil for our alignment?" a gravelly New Jersey accent crackled through his earpiece. Ant chuckled at the dungeons and dragons joke as he lifted the knife from the ground, it was a favorite hobby for himself and his Goblin companion. Almost karmically he cursed right afterward as he knew his shirt would ride up and expose his diaper.

Ant's full name was Anteros, probably the seventeenth to carry the name, though he wasn't sure if he should rightfully call himself "the seventeenth", after all the name belonged to his great uncle's line rather than his own father's. Like everyone of his father's line, he had wavy bright red hair, and piercing blue eyes that were currently covered by a rough black mask which held in place the small camera and earpiece with which he was connected to his partner. The strap for the camera/earpiece combo was always a little itchy over his high cheekbones and he briefly reached to scratch it, exposing a small sliver of bare chin before he pulled the mask back down. He was also wearing a navy blue shirt and blue pants over his slightly olive toned skin to better conceal himself in the darkness, a mini-cobra crossbow pistol strapped to his thigh, spare bolts encircling it.

Ant had spent the better part of his spring break tracking the man he currently had tied up on the floor to this abandoned building in the warehouse district of New Orleans. The man was one of the Daimones of the Sea, descendents of Triton who liked to style themselves as deities or spiritual patrons of various bodies of water, this group claiming several inlets and bayous at the mouth of the Mississippi.

"You have some information I need to know," Ant said as he stuck his knife next to the man's throat, the moonlight glinting off both the knife and the scale-like sheen that periodically broke through on the Daimone's neck. In reality Ant knew they were little more than pretentious thugs, engaging in organized crime and smuggling. "Hey, I don't know nothin, do I look like a boss to you?" his accent wasn't that far off from his companion's, "I hope you know what you're doin..." the Goblin said quietly in his ear as if on cue. It was a weird quirk of New Orleans that the accent of their oldtimers was so different than that of the rest of the region and more similar to his companion's New Jersey one.

Pushing the knife in just enough to prevent skin breakage, but definitely with enough force to make his point, "<*I mean your real boss*>" Ant replied in a native Olympian tongue. "<*I didn't know this was a family matter*>" the Daimon replied, dropping his practiced New Orleans accent in favor of his real one, a chorus of ancient greek voices from a single mouth that would have sounded very alien to any humans listening in. "<*You must be a Cupid, explains why you piss yourself, in fact I'm startin to smell somethin, I think you might want to check that, heh heh*>"

Ant pushed the knife in a little more, to draw a small amount of blood as if being nicked by a razor. "<*That's not funny*>", though Ant still sighed internally, it was a pretty good bet that he had messed when he bent over, it was always the worst when he bent over. As a Cupid, Ant had inherited many qualities from his father's line, perfect aim, strength, speed, and agility at peak human levels, but that was where the good ended as there were several possible drawbacks to being this closely related to a God. Some of his cousins got the full monty, staying forever as children and working to further Cupid's cause. Others got nothing at all and were allowed to live normal lives. But most ended up with at least one defining characteristic of being a Cupid, total incontinence.

Ant was definitely cursed with the latter, but he might be considered one of the lucky ones from a human perspective, as he still retained the strength and agility enhancements, without the child-like appearance, instead he was a tall and very lean individual. He was no Heracles, having been much more removed and therefore much more human than the legendary demigod, but he could probably give Nightwing a run for his money. Because he failed to look the part of a stereotypical cherub however, he could never pursue the family business, "taking up the bow" they called it as they would fire arrows to form new relationships, the love produced fueling the Cupid's power. Instead, Ant was pursuing a degree in Physics at a fairly low-key school that wouldn't see him get too much attention and risk exposure. Mississippi State University in the incredibly small town of Starkville, MS. But he could never quite keep himself occupied with his studies, and desired to keep involved in the family's affairs.

That was what led him here on his spring break, traveling down the Mississippi to the French Quarter in pursuit of a Daimon. To what very few parties might be concerned, he was simply enjoying some alone time to hit up Bourbon and do the normal college student things one does. But in reality he had noticed something odd going on in the forums patroned by many of his kind. Something was going down and he was going to find out what.

"<*What are they planning?*>" Ant asked. The Daimon replied, "<*I'm not high enough in rank for them to tell me anything, I'm just here to keep the offshore drilling going...*>" The other thing Ant was blessed with was an uncanny ability to tell when someone was lying, probably made the Cupids more able to tell when a relationship was working, and so he had a strong feeling the Daimon was telling the truth.

"<*You keep your nose clean, I don't want to have to go after you again*>" Ant said as he removed the knife from the Daimon's throat, and cut the ties around his ankles. "<*Rest assured Cupid, I don't wanna have to smell that again*>" the Daimon replied as he spit and awkwardly got to his feet. Ant hadn't bothered to cut the ties around his wrists.

Ant glowered at him for that comment, throwing the knife at his feet as the Daimon walked out of the abandoned warehouse. The splash as he jumped from the riverwalk told Ant he intended to travel the old fashioned way for one of his kind.

Ant followed out of the building shortly thereafter. "Well, that was a bust, eh Boss?" the Goblin asked in his ear. "No Maux, I got as much as I needed", Ant replied into the small mic as he made his way down Canal St. back towards his hotel room. While New Orleans bustled at all hours of the day, the Riverwalk was primarily a shopping district, and this time of night all the shops were closed so he was able to travel without much friction. Which Ant was thankful for as the several blocks to his hotel room were plenty friction enough with a full diaper on.

"I'm coming back in buddy, I think I need a change," Ant continued. "I'll say, that Daimon seemed like he could really smell you," Maux replied. "Shut up, your diapers don't smell so great themselves," Ant snapped back, a little annoyed at how much attention they were getting. "Mine come in a much smaller package," the Goblin retorted. "Besides boss, you weren't really gonna go through with it, were you?"

"Just playing the part for effect mon ami," Ant said, attempting to imitate the old New Orleans accent the Daimon used to defuse the tension of the question. Ant shared his partner's uneasiness with killing, but it was important to instill fear in the Daimon or he would never have gotten anything out of him.

"I'm just about there," Ant said as he saw the hotel looming above him. "I'll have you a fresh diaper ready when you get up here, d'ami," Maux replied with an almost audible wry smile.

Why would the Daimones give a damn about oil drilling? Ant thought as he entered the Mariott's front lobby…

Chapter 2

Ant's body ached as he entered the hotel room on the east end of the building. It had been a long day for him and he wasn't immortal like his fully God blooded kin. He had specifically requested an upper floor both for the view of the French Quarter, and to make it harder for retaliation if his location was discovered. Ant immediately crashed on the bed in the center of the modest room and was helped out of his diaper by Maux who assisted in the cleanup.

The short green skinned Goblin had been his companion for a few years now. He had bright red eyes, a bulbous button nose, between two large goblin ears and was currently clad in a simple t-shirt and baby diaper, this shirt featuring the logo of the Goblinoid faction of a popular dystopian tabletop wargame. Ant couldn't decide whether it was irony, per se, but it still produced a chuckle. The Goblin was from another realm, in addition to Olympus and Earth, Maux was from a dimension in which his people had experienced a great cataclysm and were forced as refugees unto another.

Ant knew Maux didn't like to go into details about what exactly happened to his family, but it was during one of Ant's travels among the realms that he came across the creature sleeping alone in an alleyway, and he naturally felt a kinship with the odd fellow due to their shared disability issues and the rest as they say, was history.

After the last few wipes were finished the Goblin removed the used diaper from the bed and placed it into a nearby trash bag that was not far from his multiple duffle bags. One might think he was staying for a month rather than the weekend, but the extra baggage was needed for his diapering supplies, which conveniently covered his combat gear for the occasional security checkpoint. These particular diapers were expensive, but worth it for when he was out on a mission, it was the only time he wore them. While the backing was plastic, the tapes were "hook and loop" systems of the same type used in the baby diapers Maux was currently wearing. It was nearly impossible to break them, which was important when feats of agility were at play. Accordingly he had already been in the practice of using baby diapers as boosters due to their cheapness compared to adult boosters, so it wasn't that great a burden to keep Maux in diapers too, which the goblin considered a great improvement over the strips of cloth employed by his kind, and since he wasn't much bigger than a human toddler anyway, Maux fit in the Size 6 just fine. In return Maux was the eyes and ears of Ant's operation, as well as general research and tech, sitting in their private chat server watching and listening to the stream as Ant conducted their operations.

After a quick shower that Ant found slightly annoying to take with the high pressure shower head employed by the hotel, he was dried and helped into a fresh diaper by Maux. A slightly cheaper and less absorbent diaper than the one he'd been changed out of, they were almost its polar opposite with a comfortable cloth backing more similar to the baby one his companion had on, but more traditional plastic landing zone tapes. Though less absorbent, it was only slightly so, and plenty for the rest of the night Ant had planned.

After putting on a t-shirt of his own featuring a different set of greenskins, a mutated warrior family of turtles, as well as returning the diaper changing favor to Maux, Anteros sat on the hotel room bed, also opting to forgo pants, and opened up his laptop, the Goblin doing the same not far away.

Popping his pacifier in his mouth, he pulled up his browser and opened up a couple of tabs. On a mission he hated for his diaper to show, and would be mortified if anyone besides Maux learned of his pacifier usage but in private Ant found it soothing and websites like ADISC, or the Adult Baby Diaper Lover Incontinence Support Community, helped him build confidence in his predicament, if only in his "civilian" life. It was a whole community of people who took pride in their diaper wearing, some by choice, others by necessity, but notably all without the shame he had been forced to contend with from the other Olympiads growing up that he didn't enjoy revisiting like most incontinence support groups tended to do.

The other tab he pulled up was the Agora, the Olympiad forums he frequented. It required a special password to enter, an ancient Olympian word meaning "I speak in public" that only those of Olympian blood were given. Ant hoped to gain some insight into what the Daimones were doing by browsing its various topics. Usually the Agora was filled with bland posts concerning family politics and squabbles. Ant was particularly notorious for involving himself in debate on the page, as Cupids were meant to "only foster love" among people. While their heritage was indeed that of Venus, Ant always felt they too quickly forgot their male line descended from Mars, the God of War. Perhaps the restlessness of Anteros was born of this inheritance, but the many generations between himself and his more famous ancestor were probably too numerous to really draw conclusions from, if any such human genome studies were even relevant to his kind.

It was in fact these debates that spurred Ant onto his current quest. The topics previously being those of philosophy and cosmology typical of a descendant of Ancient Greece, they had recently seen an upsurge in the common Political vernacular. All of a sudden American politics was all the rage on the Agora, drowning out nearly all others. The United States Presidential election of 2016 seeming to be a major focal point, with many of the Daimones taking an extremist liking to a former reality tv star who had ran that year who pushed a new radical form of conservatism. A liking that quickly gained more followers among the Olympiads many of whom pined for a more conservative era, albeit one far more ancient than any human party was likely to fathom.

Which all of course made no sense to Ant, he never bothered with human politics, and it especially didn't with regard to the oil drilling issue, after all, if the Daimones wanted to take over that industry, one would think simply pushing the enormous wealth the descendants of Neptune had access to would be the easiest method. Mankind's politics was seemingly irrelevant to such a task, at least to Ant's mind. So why support it?

Anteros never got the answer to his question. An email notification had popped up on his browser. It was an automated message from his class telling him his assignment had been graded. Ant went cold for a moment, he didn't remember any assignments for spring break, but when he logged into the online class assignments page he saw it glaring right at him. A five page paper on the ethics of social engineering that he didn't even realize was due now glowing red with the word "late" next to the title.

"Hey buddy, you okay?" Ant heard from across the room. Ant looked up to see the glowing red eyes of his companion staring across at him. "You been awful quiet boss," Maux continued. "Sorry, just realized I missed an assignment," Ant replied though it came out a bit muffled with the pacifier in.

"You wanna do some raids?" the Goblin asked rows of sharp teeth glinting in the dim light of the room, already knowing that there was no way for Ant to make up assignments in that class. "Sure," Ant replied, though he dreaded the inevitable midterm grade there was nothing he could really do about it right then, and pulled up the MMORPG frequented by he and his friend. The two of them played near perfect replicas of eachother, with Ant as a Goblin mage, and Maux playing a Human ranger.

Attempting to take his mind off of the assignment and the mission, he and the goblin played until the wee hours of the morning, when the both of them finally got too sleepy to continue, and put their night diapers on.

Chapter 3

"WHAT DO YOU WANT!? WHAT DO YOU WANT!? WHAT DO YOU WANT!?"

Anteros awoke with a jolt as the cellphone cried out in the middle of the room for his attention. As he climbed out of bed he could hear rain hitting the window of his hotel room. The awkward walk in the twilight darkness was even more perilous due to the swelling of his wet diaper and he almost tripped before he got there over his clothes and equipment.

Glass shattered as a bullet crashed into the bed where he'd just recently been sleeping. "Fuck!" he heard Maux curse as the goblin rolled off the bed and more bullets filled the mattress with a dull thump thump thump. Foam bits and springs filled the air as Ant struggled to make it to his equipment, the army crawl position being none too helped with a soggy diaper gumming up the works.

Ant felt a tape pop against the cheap rough carpeting of the hotel room floor, rain now being interlaced with wind and thunder offering an offbeat to the rhythmic thumping of the rifle's shots. *Just a little further*, he thought as landed with a thud on hard solid rock.

"What the fu-" Ant's words were cut off as a bag of diapers hit him square in the face, followed shortly by a gently descending Maux walking as if he was slowly descending a flight of stairs in mid-air. "Sorry boss, but given the circumstances I thought drastic measures may be warranted," Maux said as Anteros got to his feet beside him.

The arid desert stretched out on either side of him, they were atop a red rock cliff face punctuated only by the occasional shrubbery, the scene wouldn't have looked out of place in New Mexico or Arizona. Below them a valley gave away the fact that this was definitely not in Santa Fe, as it contained what appeared for all intents and purposes was a large bustling city until examined more closely and one realized that all of the structures were actually large animal hide tents held up by various large animal bones as scaffolding. "We should get movin though, if anyone here finds out I know magic we're boned," Maux said as Anteros realized exactly where they were. This was Maux's home realm, the city below was Olgolgarium, the Goblin refugee city. "Yeah, plus that hotel room will have a trace left in it now," Ant replied, he only used magic very sparingly as every time he did it left an almost scent-like trail that could be picked up on by other Olympiads.

Anteros then realized he was naked save for his now tape-broken diaper, which sagged even harder as apparently he'd done more than wet himself the previous night. Not an uncommon occurrence but terribly inconvenient at this very moment.

He attempted to throw on some pants as he gathered up the items strewn about the rock embankment and loaded them up into his duffles, slinging them over his shoulder as he walked, following Maux. The slower pace of the Goblin was agony while trying to hold together a broken diaper and every time a tumbleweed blew past Ant could swear his sinuses literally itched. It wasn't long before he knew he had begun to leak, the pants becoming unmistakably damp.

Ant gritted his teeth in frustration, there had been no time to get changed before departure, and no matter how many times it happened, a leak always produced a combination of shock and immediate waves of shame coalescing as an empty feeling in his chest.

Soon a lonesome tent manifested on his horizon, breaking his reverie. "This where we goin," Maux said glumly. Though he had recognized the tent city, Ant had never been in this particular part of the desert before, the interesting part of the world having been the densely populated population centers where the various other humanoids lived closer to bodies of water and filled with actual buildings that, while ancient looking by Earth standards, were miles ahead of Olgolgarium in development. But nevertheless the tone of defeat in Maux's voice was palpable and it gave Ant a very bad feeling about all this as his bare feet continued to crunch the red rock beneath his feet. He could only imagine where the little goblin must be taking him.

A slightly larger plump Goblin wearing a raggedy flower patterned garment seemingly meant to resemble a human dress was tending a garden of various plants that shown a variety of otherworldly hues like electric blues and pinks in front of the tent. As the two approached Ant could see the other goblin look up and wrinkle her nose. Almost instinctively Anteros winced, he knew what she was smelling and it was like he was in elementary all over again.

"Hello Ma," Maux said as he came to a halt outside the garden and Ant stopped cold. *Ma?* Anteros had always assumed Maux was an orphan, Ant having met him in the more central cities to the east of Olgolgarium failing to beg for change on his own. After the female goblin bent down to hug her son, she looked up at Ant and gasped. "You brought a human!? And he's covered in BLOOD!" her eyes somehow becoming even wider ruby orbs as she cried out in shock.

"Don't worry, he's with me," Maux said. "What do you mean covered in...?" Ant replied incredulously and that's when Ant bothered to look down at his bare chest for the first time since leaving their inauspicious landing site, probably due to his cherubim origins he grew virtually no hair on his body outside of his head and eyebrows, not even a beard. And right now that hairless chest was completely covered in blood. *What the shit?* Was the only thought that had time to go through his mind before Ant abruptly collapsed and blacked out.

Chapter 4

Anteros felt...off. Something didn't feel right as he rubbed the sleep from his eyes, and that's when he remembered what happened. The shooting, the escape, and his having stumbled through the desert...but it all sort of went blank from there.

Ant was laying in a makeshift bed made of rags. *Damp*, the feeling was uneasy but unmistakably there, *That's different*, he thought. Reaching down to his crotch area he realized he wasn't wearing his traditional disposable diapers, he had on a swaddling of rough cloth, and he'd wet it pretty badly.

"Good morning starshine," Ant heard a familiar gravelly voice say from the corner of the room. It was actually a pretty spacious area, though obviously a tent it was a quite large tent, with multiple sections including the one he was currently resting in. "What happened?" Ant managed to mumble out.

"Well, it was kinda funny actually, you passed out on arrival," Maux said with a bit of a chuckle. "What do you mean? The last thing I remember was seeing your...mother?" Ant replied. "Yeah, apparently you're not used to the dry air here, the blood was actually a nosebleed, by the time we got back to the tent you'd suffered a big enough loss to go lightheaded, and fainted, ya pansy!" Maux guffawed. "Shut up!" Ant said, flipping him the bird.

"Heh, I'm glad you're alright though. Gave me a bit of a scare for a minute there, boss," Maux said with a bit of a smile, hopping down to sit beside him on the pallet of rags.

"The fuck am I wearing?" Ant asked, gesturing at his wet cloth diaper. "Well, Ma doesn't believe in using humanoid tech so she refused to figure out your diapers, and opted to do you like she'd do me. It's called a spargana, I don't think you really wanna know what it's made of," Maux said, at which point Ant saw the brown leathery hide wrapping his Goblinoid companion.

"Good, you are awake," Ant heard Maux's mother say as she entered the bedding area of her tent dwelling. "And I see you have about as much control as my son here, tsk-tsk," and she moved closer to the bedding, another of the leathery diapers in hand. "Come, I change you," she said, leaning in. "Uh, Ma? Maybe I should do it? Ant might be more comfortable in one of his own diapers..." but before Maux had even gotten the sentence out, his mother had already begun unfolding the spargana from Ant's diaper area.

He didn't have it in him to resist and let the old goblin do her work, and he was thankful that he hadn't messed again in his sleep. The roughness of the material against his bare skin felt a bit like having a sofa on his crotch, but there wasn't a whole lot he could do about it at the moment. "There, all better," she said as she smiled at her handiwork. Ant's stomach gargled a deafening roar reminding him why he hadn't had any solids in his diaper. There were no solids in his belly either.

"Worry not for hunger. I make stew," she said as Anteros sat up on the pallet and she exited the room. "Well boss, I tried," Maux said solemnly. "I know you did buddy, but...well, I wanted to say it's not so bad, but the chafe's already feeling a bit awful," and the both of them laughed at that. There were so many questions Ant had for Maux at this point. What happened to his father? Why didn't he ever talk about his mother? Did he have any other family? Ant was achingly curious but he didn't dare ask and risk violating his friend's trust. He would tell him the details in due time. Instead, Anteros settled on something a bit more benign, if no less serious. "Why are you afraid to do Magic here? I know I'm afraid of being caught by snooping Olympiads, what's your excuse?"

"Well, I'm er not supposed ter do magic, strictly speaking," Maux said with a grin, quoting the half giant from the children's book. But his grin quickly turned to a grimace as Maux continued, "I suppose I should've told you this sooner, and I guess there's no point keeping it to myself now. There's just a lot of hurt in it, you know?" "What do you mean?" Ant said inquisitively. "It's my fault, Ant. All of it. It's because of me, because they were cursed with…ME!" Maux replied, gesturing down at his diaper as he did so. "Goblins aren't supposed to know magic, at least, not supposed to know my kind of magic. Every Goblin is illiterate, and because I'm not, my father is dead and my mother lives out here in squalor. I couldn't take it and I ran away."

"Well..that does sound awfully terrible," Ant said adopting a grimace of his own, "but I'm not seeing how it's your fault exactly."

"Because of these..because of this!" Maux said, once again gesturing at the spargana around his waist and the growing wet spot therein. "Goblin males are meant to be warriors, but it was impossible for me to become a warrior. I'm small even for other greenskins, and I never could stop pissing and shitting myself!" Ant winced at Maux's harshness, he could practically still hear the Daimon thug saying the same thing. And from the looks of things Maux was literally hearing it, as he stared off into space for an audible pause, reliving some past trauma in his life.

"My father still had high hopes for me though!" Maux continued when he snapped out of it, starting to brighten a little more as he clearly admired his father. "He noticed my supposed intelligence from a very early age," and were it not for Ant's waiting on the other shoe to drop in that story he'd almost envy that admiration.

"He had a radical idea. One that he thought would revolutionize the tribes. He intended to break our oldest taboo. The written word is evil to a Goblin, Ant. It steals the thoughts from your mind, it eats your soul from within. At least that's how the superstition goes. The penalty for reading is death. But my father wanted to try to teach me. During the raids on human encampments, he would steal their scrolls and manuscripts and bring them home to me."

"I devoured them, every single one," Maux said with a sanguine smile, "The stories were the best ones, could imagine being anywhere but the tent I was confined to as a knight or an adventurer or whatever. But my father was most impressed when he saw I'd learn spells. He figured if the tribes saw the power in the magic I'd learned that they'd have to accept me!"

The saddest laugh Ant ever heard escaped his friend's lips as tears began to stream down his face. "But no amount of power or weaponry was going to change them. The Gods demanded death for his crimes, and they gave it to 'em," Maux continued, the bitter anger and resolve in his voice as his eyes stared daggers into the bedding below him. "The tribes raided our tent and killed my father, he fought hard till the end though, gave Ma and me just enough time to escape with a portal he made me summon."

"I ain't been able to forgive myself since," Maux finished as Ant reached out to console him with a hug and-

-a bullet whizzed right past his ear. *What the shit?* "Fuck they fou-!" and the rest of Maux's sentence was drowned out by the sound of ceramic bowls crashing to the floor. This time Ant wasn't going down without a fight, and he reached down into his bag on the floor by the pallet, pulling out his crossbow pistol and a couple of bolts.

Loading one up as another bullet zipped by, he strode out of the tent through the side exit flap, figuring whoever was shooting at him was aiming for what passed as a door. Taking aim he finally got a good look at his assassin. He was truly massive, at least two meters tall, and when he saw the attacker's face he imperceptibly shook with fear, a wet spot of his own appearing on his leather diaper. His attacker possessed a single large eye, currently with a telescopic lens attached. Descendants of Neptune, there could be no doubt this was related to his recent conflict with the Daimones, but that they would go so far as to attack him in broad daylight...

Ant had no time to dwell on it, his own aim being of Godly origin and telescopic in its own right, leveling out the pistol he squeezed the trigger and fired, directly at the attached lens on the Cyclops.

His shot connected and a flash banged off the Cyclopic face on impact. But that was when Ant felt a monstrous tug on his biceps as he was thrown back into the tent. Maux's mother now standing before him, eyes glowing red as chaotic energies cackled around her. "Go, now!" was all she said before beginning to mutter an incantation. "Ma, NO!" Maux cried out, "I can't leave you!"

"Go, I take care of self!" the older Goblin said as a portal opened just outside the bed pallet, and Ant's bags and items were sucked in along with Maux. "Which one of you motherfuckers blinded me!?" the Cyclops bellowed, as Ant's larger weight held him in place just long enough to hear the greenskin's response, "Nobody, nobody at all."

And the tent and the old goblin blinked out of existence just as Ant was sucked into the portal himself.

Chapter 5

Ant fell on top of his friend with a hard thud, and it felt like just in time too, as the modest dorm room was chilled to the core, icy fog covering the windows, and icicles forming a small circle in the floor. Maux struggled free from beneath him tears streaming down his face from his similarly red glowing eyes showing with an intensity Ant had never seen on his companion before.

"I'll kill him! He's dead! I'm-!!!" and before the Goblin could cast his frost magic and make a huge mistake Ant grabbed hold of him and embraced him as hard as he could. "MMMLETMMMMEMMMGOOO" the Goblin struggled to break free. "It's gonna be okay buddy, I swear Maux, I saw her, she got away, it's gonna be okay it's gonna be okay," and slowly Maux's breathing slowed and they just sat there for a moment as the heat began to kick on in the small apartment complex.

"It's gonna be okay," Ant said again after the long pause. "She got out, you saw it?" Maux asked as his eyes dimmed to their familiar pearlescent red. "Yeah, right after casting the portal she teleported out," Ant said.

Maux sighed, "I didn't even know she knew magic, man. She must've been studying while I was gone. I'm even more worried about her now."

"Yeah, well, you almost had all of Neptune's realm bearing down on us just then," Ant said as Maux looked around the room surveying the ice currently dripping out of existence as the apartment slowly returned to room temperature.

"Sorry boss. S'pose I was a bit distraught," Maux replied with a slight chuckle, but Antcros could tell that he was still drowning in worry, just now compounded with worry that he almost brought everyone else down with him.

The next few hours passed in relative silence. Ant didn't know how she did it, but Maux's mother had ported him to their dorm room in Starkville. It was the tail end of Spring Break, meaning it was still cold in these parts, so nobody would be too suspicious of the sudden drop in temperature. Ant could only hope that because Maux hadn't got the spell off that the trace wouldn't be triggered, but he had no real way of knowing that until someone popped up on his doorstep.

Instead all he could do was get changed into a more conventional diaper, doing the same in kind for Maux. It was always a soothing experience for them both to get out of a wet diaper and into a dry one, and that was all the more so with the sparganas they had been wearing previously. Ant would never take modern tech for granted again.

After he got done putting his supplies back into their various storage containers, next to the clear ones containing his diaper supply, and arranging his action figures and vinyl figures and other various nerdy trinkets from things as diverse as Power Rangers, to Dungeons and Dragons, to Wrestling as he liked to do every so often, he grabbed his pacifier, popped it in, and sat at his desktop computer.

When his phone finished charging he had several notifications, not least of which were the messages from his mother. Ant's father never paid him much attention, after all, Ant wasn't a prized cherub like he was and therefore didn't rate much in his view. But his mother was human and cared about him greatly, often more than Ant really would have liked. Especially now as she seemed altogether too upset that Ant hadn't called and that she had access to the online classroom app the school used and saw he'd missed an assignment.

It took some convincing to get her to accept that he was okay and that he'd just forgotten his phone charger when he was out with some friends. The fact that by some miracle this meant Ant had made a friend seemed to brighten her spirits somewhat and that aided his attempts to metaphorically beat her off with a stick.

With that accomplished, Ant turned to the task at hand, scouring the Agora to confirm whether he'd been identified. Fortunately, the human news media seemed to be pointing the blame on a "lone gunman" and the overall discussion centered around whether this should change the country's gun laws than anything relevant to Ant or his situation. While Ant didn't believe in killing or guns as a general rule, he didn't believe in getting into Human politics even more. Being a child of Gods, he'd always found himself a bit aloof when it came to pure humans in a general sense.

The Olympiads knew that the attack was actually related to them, but the Cyclops hadn't been given the name of his target, only that it was a Cupid and it was in New Orleans. Naturally there was a lot of suspicion thrown towards Neptune's line as the Cyclops descended from it, but the fact that he took jobs in a mercenary fashion seemed to be enough to pacify anyone trying to take up the scent.

Ant decided he needed to lay low for a while. For the next several weeks he focused on his schoolwork. He was taking several math intensive classes and solving the various problems involved was a pretty good distraction for a while. He managed to pull Bs out despite what his escapade had cost him. But through it all he could tell that he and Maux were spending less and less time as pals, the Goblin's mind constantly filled with worry over the whereabouts of his mother. Ant wished he could help him but he had no idea how to get in touch with her without bringing down the whole world upon him, and it was clear Ant had made some enemies with powerful people.

The pattern of Ant leaving for class, coming home, getting his diaper changed, leaving again, then coming back for another change and homework and internet repeated itself ad nauseum until one day out of the blue, just as the weather was starting to warm back up, a miniscule portal opened up just above his currently overfilled diaper pail and spit out a letter scrawled on parchment.

I did not risk contacting you until I was certain we weren't going to be followed. I hope you don't mind that I have been keeping tabs on you since you left, I learned to read and write from your scrolls and enough magic to trace your whereabouts, but I dared not risk showing you for fear that you'd worry. But I guess the squig is out of the sack now. I'm doing fine, I simply moved my tent to a new plot deep in the woods of Azurefel. But I've been keeping track of the Cyclops since we last departed and I think you should come and see me. Something is not right.

I love you my boy,
Ma

Ant noted that her syntax was a lot more efficient when she was writing than when she was speaking, but this thought was quickly dispelled by the growing pit deep in his stomach. He'd read it without even thinking about it, but he really shouldn't have done so, it should have went to Maux first.

"Boss? What's up?" and Ant hesitated for a minute as he try to imagine an apology in his mind but everything sounded like a hollow and empty excuse to him. "It's a letter from your mother," was all Anteros could muster as he braced for impact.

"SHE'S OKAY!?" and Maux leapt from the bed and almost tackled Ant as he grabbed the letter, "Wow! I'm so impressed she's picked up writing this well!" Maux said brightly, clearly relieved as an almost visible weight seemed to disappear from his shoulders. Ant sighed with relief too, he was afraid he'd pissed his friend off, but then the pit reappeared in his stomach as he realized he couldn't just let it go that easily either.

"I'm so happy and relieved too buddy, I'm sorry I didn't immediately hand it to you, it was almost instinctual that I read it," Ant said, attempting to apologize.

"I don't even care, I'm just so happy knowing she's alive!" Maux said, practically jumping up and down, diaper sagging as clearly he'd dropped a bit of a load in his excitement. "Well, I'm sorry nonetheless, let's get you cleaned up bro," and Ant went to grab one of his baby diapers out of a sterilite.

Maux could barely hold still as Anteros untaped the soiled diaper and grabbed his wipes, powder, and rash ointment to get the little Goblin cleaned up. Tossing it into the trash, he carefully taped on a new one as they both sat up just staring at the letter for a moment.

Mail across realms wasn't as simple as typing up an email or sealing an envelope, it required some specialized magic. But it was common enough among the Olympiads that typically it wouldn't raise any eyebrows. But getting the two of them and enough diapers and supplies to Azurefel? That would get them caught faster than his favorite video game rodent could run.

They would have to go the old fashioned way.

Chapter 6

The next day Ant had his bags packed with enough diapers for a three day trip, since he didn't know what the old Goblin needed the two of them for, and exited his apartment building with Maux in tow, currently dressed as a human toddler, complete with a tiny beanie concealing his ears, and a footed onesie keeping his three toed feet from being visible to the outside world. Only if someone got in real close could they tell it was actually a Goblin following close behind Ant, and Maux had gotten very good over the years at playing the part of an extremely shy baby and holding in close to Ant's legs when other people were around.

They walked to a grimy bus stop at the end of the road connecting their dorm complex to the University and the rest of Starkville. He'd printed out a bus ticket that would take them on the roughly five hour bus ride to Belle Chasse, La. Although Maux would inevitably need to be changed in the Bus Passenger restroom, Ant himself had put on a diaper with a modified baby diaper as a booster in the hopes that he wouldn't need to get changed until they arrived, but he'd had no such luck and about half way there was forced to enter the uncomfortable stall and clean himself to replace his soiled diaper. There was a brief moment as he'd struggled in the tiny on board bathroom to get the job done that somebody might wonder what he was up to or notice a smell, but the overall noise of the bus and the, let's face it, sheer smell of the bus itself drowned out anything his body could add to it.

Once they'd arrived Ant paid a ridesharing service to take him out to a place in the middle of nowhere near the mouth of the Mississippi River. Here Ant was going to engage in some complicated magic, a spell that would open up a gateway to another realm via the old ways and he didn't want anyone snooping around while he was getting it done.

With Maux's help he managed to get on his swim diaper cover. It wasn't absorbent enough to have on for longer than a few minutes if one wasn't going to get in the water, as it was primarily designed to contain solid waste, but it was better than having a diaper swell up on him in the water. He'd experienced that more than he'd like already.

The spell was risky, it could only be performed at the mouths of great waterways. Famously it'd been encountered by the hero Ulysses at the modern day Rock of Gibraltar to enter into the Underworld, of course he'd done it accidentally. But if Ant wasn't careful he could end up in any number of worlds in transit, or worse, gulping down the river Lathe and forgetting who he was, and since he wasn't dead he'd be cursed to wander the Underworld until Hades dealt with him or his soul was torn apart by the wraiths of the undead who had yet to find the peace to drink from the waters themselves.

As Ant waded out into the waters he could feel the cold surrounding him, the muddy river floor felt oddly like tapioca between his toes. The water this close to the Gulf of Mexico was more brackish than fresh, the added salt filled his nostrils as he breathed in deep to steady his nerves and his resolve. The sky was overcast and it wasn't quite into Spring long enough for it to start getting warm, even this far south.

On the shore Maux was busy arranging ingredients in a circle. He drew roughly one liter of water into an empty plastic bottle, placed a small container of ashes to serve as carbon, various other containers containing ammonia , lime, phosphorus, salt, saltpeter, sulfur, fluorine, iron, silicon, and a few other trace elements. The value of a good apothecary knows no bounds. Not in high enough quantities to conjure the real thing, but enough to get a functional facsimile for Anteros' purposes here. The problem with porting to a location as is more typical of transportation among the realms, is that like any other magic, it leaves a trace. A portal even worse as it leaves a door that can easily be opened. Anteros could not risk that or else this visit to Maux's mother would end exactly the same as last time, or worse.

Instead Ant needed a way of metatravel that did not rely upon magical means. Ant knew of only a few beings with the ability, and only one that might not kill him on the spot. It was summoning him that was the trick.

Clouds began to darken the sky above them, lightning cracking as Maux began to chant ancient Olympian around the circle, the faint glow of his eyes transitioning to a blindingly blistering red, this time accompanied with an eerily unsettling smile as the magic began to coalesce around his Goblin frame. Though Ant remained in the middle of the bayou with his eyes closed, had he been able to see it the circle would have appeared to open up as a black cartoon hole in the ground, then filled with the entire spectrum of light as if the static of an old television set.

As the lightning and thunder built to a crescendo Maux raised his hands in the air and slammed them down upon the ground as lightning struck the hole and then as abruptly as it started the clouds disappeared and the sun shone brightly as the magic induced storm pushed the moisture out of the sky. When the smoke cleared on the circle all of the containers were vaporized and in their place a human cadaver rested. One might mistake it for a mannequin were it not for its fleshy feeling to the touch, it had no organs or facial features, it was, in effect, a placebo for the being Ant had summoned.

An unnatural fog surrounded Ant despite the clear skies as a creaky boat nearly collided with him before stopping on a dime unlike any boat in existence. It was a long and wooden gondola, charred black. On it stood a slender old man, with scraggly gray beard and hair, wearing a simple black robe.

"<*I need a favor*>" Anteros stated simply in his native tongue, trying to keep the fear from escaping his voice. Charon, the ferryman, was known for beating people with his long oar currently stuck in the side of the river into submission, forcing them to enter the realm of the dead, living or no. But Anteros was an Olympiad, and as such afforded certain privileges, though he certainly wouldn't be the first demigod who'd had those privileges rescinded by the old ferryman.

Charon held aloft his hand, and Maux, carrying Ant's duffle bags instantly blinked out of existence and reappeared in the boat in front of the old man. Reaching out with his small clawed fingers, the goblin placed two American Eagle Palladium coins into the aloft hand. Any favor that didn't end with Ant on the wrong side of the river Styx required payment, but the ferryman didn't exactly take the full faith and credit of the United States Government, nor any human government for that matter. He needed something more real. Ant hoped the rarer metal would win him some support here, it was certainly worth a lot more than the $25 it said on the tin.

Charon nodded simply, and placed the coins in his robe. Maux grinned, the spell had worked, and the trouble they'd gone to in acquiring the coins had been worth and if any Olympiad noticed the trace all he'd find is a husk of a cadaver, decaying at an unnaturally fast rate. Ant then climbed into the gondola, but then grimaced as the effort brought more with it than the water he was dripping. As the boat pulled off, unnaturally steady even in the comparatively calm waters of the Mississippi sound, Maux sighed and began to help him out of the swim diaper, drying him off with a towel they'd packed on board.

The ferryman didn't even spare a glance their way, looking unceasingly towards the horizon, the things he'd seen from sinners and saints of all stripes(all shared death equally) meant that a diaper change certainly wasn't about to faze him. Ant went red as he was laid down on the bottom of the gondola and had to be wiped clean in broad daylight. Though nobody could see him under the veil of the dead, the knowledge that he had to be diapered in front of the legendary Charon was humiliating. It was a wonder any of the Cupids could be taken seriously as members of their race.

Finishing up with the wiping Maux placed the dirty swim diaper into a plastic bag that he tied and placed inside the duffle bag. The goblin figured it prudent to use one of his mission diapers for the trip over. Ant hated when he had to place the used ones in his duffle though, fighting the smell permeating his bags was a constant struggle, and each and every time a soiled diaper was placed in it was like taking on a smelly debt in his mind.

After wiping his front and applying rash cream and powder, Maux taped the hook and loop system in place, and Ant rose and was helped into his pants, the soft padding feeling nice against his skin especially compared to the cold and clammy water he'd exited. Ant then checked Maux, but the baby diaper he'd been wearing was actually designed for capacity, rather than the swim diaper Ant had been wearing so he wasn't quite ready for a change yet.

The boat was proceeding at a blinding speed, the dead were often said to see flashes of their previous lives in the blur of color rushing past the gondola. Ant wasn't dead, however, and as the boat exited the Gulf of Mexico and into the Atlantic all he could see was a lot of water.

The boat ride passed in complete silence, Maux likely trying to process the new knowledge of the literacy of his mother, and Ant was too socially awkward to make decent conversation in the best of circumstances, let alone with the impossibly ancient God currently steering their vessel.

Ant's eyes started to droop, it had been a long day for him, and the static scenery wasn't exactly riveting viewing. After a couple of times jolting himself awake he finally drifted off to sleep...

Chapter 7

The water was still around him. The boat had come to a dead stop and Ant found himself alone on a completely still sea surrounding him in all directions. A cold empty pit grew in his stomach as he didn't see Maux anywhere, the ferryman was gone, he truly was alone. Panic began to creep its way in his mind, he had no idea how to get home or which direction home was even in, somewhere in the back of his mind the fact that his supplies were all gone spoke up right as he felt a warm spot in his diaper area and an all too familiar sinking feeling as the stream poured down his legs and into the boat below.

He didn't even have time to curse as a massive tentacle smashed off the front of the boat, splinters flying in all directions. A truly titanic individual rose from the depths below. Half man, half various forms of sea life, his long beard seemed to be made of seaweed and algae, and his skin was the color of pond scum. From beneath his crown of shells he glowered down at the cupid below him, pointing his trident straight at the chest of Anteros and blowing his conch shell, producing a wave that brought the gondola at eye level.

Ant found himself unable to scream, and it was only right then that it hit him that something was off about this whole thing. No noise, no sound at all, nothing. Each event had occurred with himself filling in the blanks where sound effects should have been. *This is all a dream*, he thought. *No…a message*, they were in Neptune's domain, but this manifestation of his son, and the father of the Daimones, Triton, was artificial. The real thing wouldn't dare spark a war by attacking Charon, Hades would exact his vengeance if they were dumb enough to try that. Anteros still retained enough of his family faith to believe that to be the case.

Though unable to make sound escape his lips, Anteros glowered defiantly at the fishman, he wasn't going to be intimidated. Pointing two fingers at his eyes and then pointing right back at the creature before him, Ant smirked as he felt a hard slap in the face.

"Wake up buddy!" Maux cried out as Ant tried to shake the sleep from his eyes. Ant felt down to his crotch area, he was wet but he didn't leak, and he mouthed a silent offering of thanks that that part of the vision hadn't come to pass.

"Sorry, I must've fallen asleep," Ant left it at that, however, unwilling to risk his suspicions going through the grapevine and making it to Neptune's ears just yet.

Charon raised a bony gnarled finger as the boat entered the domain of the underworld, and hundreds of portals splayed out all before him. All of them a seeming mirror offering a window into another world. Ant glanced from one to another trying to match his image of the Azurefel forest he had in his mind's eye.

Ant began to despair that he'd missed it and had no idea how to convince him to turn around when he saw it flash right before him, the distinctive purple foliage covered in various hues of purple fungus, the mushroom caps offering a dead give away that it was the forest he was after.

Without even having to gesture, the boat pulled off into the portal. Anteros should've known better than to worry, the ferryman could see into the hearts of men, and he knew what Anteros needed without any asking required. As the boat disappeared into the world between worlds, and Anteros reappeared beside Maux and his bags beside a particularly sticky redcap-esque mushroom, Ant attempted to thank the ferryman for his help, but he and the boat were already gone, onto the next soul in need of transport.

Anteros shouldered the duffels and trudged down the footbeaten path deeper into the fungal forest. The flora was an amazing sight to behold, fungal blooms of all shapes and sizes splayed out before him, broad mushroom formations taking the place of leaves, and the canopy was so thick there was no way to tell whether it was day or night, but all glowed with an otherworldly purple hue given off by the bioluminescent growths sprouting from all corners of the forest before them.

Ant marveled at the sight, the exotic locales were his favorite part of travelling between worlds. As their steps down the beaten path got heavier Ant started to fear they were lost. He figured that anyone trying to make their home in the fungal forest would probably be close to the path so as not to get even more lost than he and his goblin companion already were.

Come to think of it Maux hadn't said two words since they'd landed, and he was only hearing one set of footsteps....*Oh fuck*!

Ant jerked his head around in all directions, "Maux!" he didn't hear any response. He started running back down the path, he wasn't going to lose him, not now! "Maux!" Panic was starting to set in, he'd failed his friend. Ant would never be able to forgive himself, "MAUX!"

"Hahaha, stop it, stop it! It tickles!" the New Jersey esque accent reached Ant's ears just before he rounded a corner next to a particularly tall toadstool and found his friend rolling around on the ground being...sniffed? Licked? How do animate fungi interact with the environment? The creature looked like a walking set of reeds, but with a lot of unmistakably fungal stems and caps sticking out of the ends, one of which was currently nudging his goblin not unlike that of a nosy puppy.

"Dude, what the hell? I thought I'd lost you!" Ant cried out when he'd found him. "Ha, I'm sorry Boss, haha, he tackled me!" Maux said, tears beginning to stream down his face. "Come on, shoo!" Ant called out attempting to sweep away the critter.

"Thanks buddy," Maux said with some exasperation as Ant helped him to his feet. "I thought I was a goner!" Maux quipped with some mock anxiety. "I'm sure your diaper definitely was," Ant said with an eyeroll, as Maux felt around his crotch area and scowled. "Tickles are the worst," Maux said with a grimace, and Ant chuckled.

"Come on, let's get out of here, I'll change you when we get to your mother's," Ant said as a long shadow crept over the bioluminescent clearing. "Did it just get darker?" Maux said, as a version of the reedpuppy loomed behind them like some sort of giant reedbear.

"Run"

Ant didn't know whether he said it, Maux said it, or if they both did but he took off in the opposite direction of the reedbear as fast as he could stride, fresh fungal growth and chitinous root systems crushing beneath his feet with sickening crunch with each hard step. He almost sprinted too fast for his friend to keep up so he grabbed him by the shirt and Maux instinctively crawled up his arm and onto his shoulder.

Grabbing his crossbow pistol from the holster on his leg with his other arm, Ant pointed it at the creature chasing them, the problem is, he didn't know what to aim for. The Cupids have perfect aim, otherworldy, godly perfect aim. But none of that meant a godsdamned thing if the thing you're shooting at lacked a face or general torso or much of any discernible body parts at all.

This is bad, he thought as he just squeezed the trigger in the general direction of the thing's center and fired off a bolt. The bolt was a flashbang of the type he'd fired at the Cyclops, but while blinding a one-eyed thug made perfect sense, there was really nothing to blind on a fungus, Ant could only hope it pulled enough of a distraction as the resounding bang ricocheted off the surrounding environment.

The smell of pungent grilled mushrooms filled the air, the reedbear had smacked his arrow out of the air and directly into a resting toadstool, but the smell of the burning chitin seemed to have a calming effect on the creature, and the heads of the reeds wrapped around the large mushroom. At least now Ant had an answer as to what the original reed creature had been trying to do to Maux, he'd been sizing him up for a meal. It seemed a lot less cute in that context, but Anteros didn't have a lot of time to dwell on it anyway.

"Y-you wanna let me down now, Boss?" Maux said his voice still a little shaky from the ordeal. "Sorry Buddy," Ant replied as he leaned down for his companion to depart. "Suppose I was a bit distracted," he continued. "Can't imagine why," Maux observed wryly as he stole one last glance at the reedbear enjoying a large meal.

The rest of the trudging passed by rather uneventful, after a couple of hours of walking they both needed a diaper change, and stopped off at a particularly large green mushroom that they both laughed about giving them extra lives to get said diaper change.

But the change didn't happen, as Maux was about to climb onto the top of the cap, Anteros saw a flickering light just beyond the edge of the path. "Um, Ant? I'm feeling a bit exposed up here," Maux said, as Ant had taken the goblin's pants, but hadn't gotten to the untape diaper step quite yet.

"I think we should do it inside actually..." Ant said, as he started walking off the path and towards the flickering light. "Inside?" Maux questioned as he hopped off the mushroom and when he saw it he ran into the clearing, wet diaper sagging between his legs. "Ma! It's me!" but they both stopped dead before the goblin got any response.

Maux's mother was there alright, but she was tied to a yellow hued, tree sized, mushroom across the way from a flickering fire, next to which sat a large, burly, Cyclops, a telescopic lens strapped to his forehead.

"*<took you longer than I'd thought it would,>*" the Cyclops said in the native Olympian. "*<I really thought I'd see someone who bested me in combat much sooner. It's quite the embarrassment really,>*"

Ant's blood ran cold and an empty void filled the pit of his stomach. *The trace...*of course! They were so thrilled to hear Maux's mother survived that they hadn't stopped to consider at all whether any of it was true. The letter must have been written by the Cyclops who instead of jumping through the portal to gods only knew where, followed Maux's mother and laid a trap.

"*<Azurefel is far enough off the beaten track to keep any prying eyes away while I finish you off,>*"

"You're damned right it is..." and that was when Ant saw one of the more disturbing sights he'd ever seen. Maux had a horrific smile across his face as he said the words, the sharp teeth forming a grinning wall from ear to ear as his eyes glowed the brightest red he'd ever seen them, his fangs filled mouth glinting in the firelight. The temperature dropped hard, frost formed on the caps of the mushrooms as the fire flickered to its death before them and Maux raised his arms to the heavens and brought them down as hundreds of icy meteorites the size of beachballs rained down from the canopy, crashing hard upon the Cyclops before he had time to react.

Ant then moved to make sure he wouldn't have any at all as he loaded up a bolt into his crossbow and whispered a spell of his own, figuring the magical cat was out of the bag at this point. Firing it straight at the Cyclops' feet, the arrow covered the ground in a sticky blue goop that would hold the beast in place while the ice continued to pummel.

Ant was loading up another arrow when the fungus began to rumble beside them, followed by audible cracks and pulls as the reedbear bounded into the clearing and tackled the Cyclops down.

Ant didn't want to think about what happened next to the Cyclops as he ran past and untied the older goblin from the yellow mushroom...trunk? Ant really needed to brush up on his biology. She was unconscious and she was ungodly heavy for something that was only four feet tall, but he managed to heave her, that was unfortunately accompanied by a smell he equally didn't want to think about. *Every fricken time!* He cursed to himself.

Anteros then sounded off a portal spell that would take them back to his apartment, not even caring about the consequences at this point. The only thing on his mind was how to save Maux's mother.

"Maux! Snap out of it, we gotta go!" Ant yelled out as the Goblin, standing over the bottom half of his body, looked about ready to eat what was left of the Cyclops himself as Ant leapt through the portal, landing face first on his apartment floor, many pounds of Goblin resting on his shoulder as her son landed just next to Ant on the rough hewn carpet.

Chapter 8

What do you do for a Goblin that needs hospital care?

That was the thought on Anteros mind after immediate needs of water and diaper changes were taken care of. He almost considered having Maux conjure some healing refreshment, but Ant couldn't be sure they wouldn't be watched, it wouldn't be long until the Daimones figured out their assassin was dead, and the Cyclops was a cousin too so they would definitely not be pleased.

For now Maux was trying to nurse her back to health with cans of chicken noodle soup. Ant briefly considered asking his mother for help, she had access to the alchemical markets in the French Quarter and could send in some health potions. Whereas Anteros was stuck in Starkville. Not exactly ground zero for alchemical success stories.

A moment of homesickness passed through Ant. His mother was from Collins, MS, but she'd met Ant's father on holiday in NOLA, a prime destination for Cupids looking to ply their trade in North America, and occasionally as had been the case for his mother, pursue hookups of their own in the magical guise of adult humans. Like most of his kind though, his father only stuck around long enough to find out Ant wasn't destined to become a Cherub and moved on. Gods were fickle and that foot of growth Ant experienced was all that Cupid needed to know. Nonetheless Ant's mother was proud of the fact that her son could trace his lineage among the gods, and ensured that he'd known ancient Olympian, his family history, and could proudly display his own Olympiad heritage. What she didn't want was him abusing his position and connections in a party town like she did, so Ant was cursed to spend his college years at Mississippi State University in the middle of nowhere.

Well, cursed wasn't quite the right word, he had a nominal amount of school pride(though football made absolutely no sense to him), and there was a cafe all the students went to for breakfast that was to die for, but Ant couldn't help but long for the urban adventures he'd left behind in New Orleans. More than once Maux suggested that longing was the real reason for his "missions". But Starkville lacked even a decent arcade! Let alone a big retro one like the Oceanwave Arcade(the irony of the name in his current situation was not lost on him) he'd frequented.

The moment passed as Ant really dreaded the talking to he'd receive if his mother ever found out what he'd been up to. There was also the fear that someone would come in and see the old goblin and while Maux was capable of hiding easily enough(Ant suspected he rather enjoyed it, as it let him play the trickster straight out of human folklore), his thick mother was going to stick out like a sore thumb. Fortunately Ant didn't have a roommate, his mother had spared him that indignity as the one thing his father did provide for him was a college fund that paid for his living space, it literally wasn't much considering the vast sums of wealth the Cupids had access to that Ant and his mother were barred from, but considering his status as a failed experiment Ant could probably consider himself lucky he got anything at all. But what a lack of roommate didn't spare him from were inspections, pest control, and a whole host of other nosy entities that had plenty of authority to barge into his dorm without announcement.

"Boss-no, Ant," Maux spoke up, breaking Anteros from his reverie, "I need to ask you something, as a friend…" and when Ant saw the pain in his companion's voice he realized how selfish he was even thinking this way. "I-I know buddy," Ant replied and the two nodded in silent understanding as they had both put two and two together. Ant sighed, he'd been worried about being chewed out by his mother, but Maux was worrying about his own mother's very life. Ant felt like a dick.

The realization of how much of a shit person he was hit him with a massive void in his chest. It was the only way, Maux's mother's injuries were magical in nature, they wouldn't heal on their own, and they couldn't risk conjuring anything themselves without putting everyone in the complex in danger via the trace.

But still, he really didn't want to do it. When his mother first learned about Maux and the fact that Ant was brazenly traveling via portals in full detection of other Olympiads her fury had been legendary. It's what originally prompted him to limit his missions to his own reality until recent events forced his hand. The disastrous results of those events forced him to conclude the wisdom of her position.

Cursing himself internally he reluctantly pulled up "Mama" on his Contacts list and hit call.

"YOU DID WHAT!?" the scream was audible from the other side of the room as Ant tried to fumble an explanation for his actions. "I-I'm sorry, we were attacked, we didn't have a choice!" Ant tried but it was only met with shouts of "ARE YOU CRAZY!?" and "ARE YOU ACTUALLY INSANE!? YOU COULD'VE BEEN KILLED!"

"She's gonna die..." Ant said softly and his mother got quiet. "Fine, I'll come up with the health potions. But we're going to have a talk when I get up there."

She hung up at that, clearly furious. Anteros hadn't told her about why he was attacked exactly, merely a lame excuse that he'd shot his mouth off at some Daimones and it spilled over into Maux's mother's dimension. It was as close to the truth as Ant was willing to give, he couldn't risk her trying to stop him.

The time when she hung up was three in the afternoon. Time worked a little differently in other pockets of reality, and what felt like half a day he'd spent wandering around the Azurfel forest had only been a couple of hours in his own time.

The next several hours passed in relative silence, Maux's entire attention was focused on keeping his mother stable. Ant serving as gopher as best as he could, fetching wet washcloths, water, anything the Goblin might need.

It was nearly dark by the time the knock sounded at the apartment door. Maux didn't even move as he held the washcloth over his mother's forehead. Anteros strode as confidently as he could to the door under the circumstances. There were few people that could elicit true fear out of Ant, one of them was recently eaten by a weird fungal creature, another was standing on the other side of this door.

"Hello mama," Ant said as nonchalantly as possible as he opened the door. "Where is she?" was all his mother said, which rather relieved him that he wasn't about to get an earful, but then made him kick himself again for thinking it was all about himself again. *Really gotta work on that,* Ant thought. Ant's mother was a bit shorter than himself, though certainly not cherub sized, probably around five foot flat, making her about a foot and change shorter than Ant himself, with long brown hair, green eyes that seemed to shift to grey depending on the orientation of the light, with a slightly overweight frame that seemed to enhance her cuteness more than make her look fat.

"She's over here," said a somewhat pitiful Maux in the corner of the room on Ant's bed(Maux himself actually preferred to curl up in an oversized dog bed underneath), were it not for the heavily breathing goblin on it, one might have even described Ant's bed as "cute", it had sheets and covers from the American adaptation of a Japanese kids superhero show, as well as several stuffed animals, many of whom were diapered, including a stuffed Goblin that looked not unlike Maux himself that Ant chuckled at when he bought it.

Right now those were all sitting in the actual wall corner while Maux's mother was positioned so that her head was raised against the wall. It was the first time since she'd arrived that Ant allowed himself to really look over her wounds. She had several deep scars in her forehead, probably where she'd been subdued by the Cyclops. Ant's mother poured the red bubbling liquid into the Goblin's mouth and it seemed to rouse her slightly but the damage was too great for the health potion to do it alone and so a small bleu cheese-like brick was pulled from Ant's mother's purse and placed into the Goblin's mouth along with the remaining health potion.

There was no healthbar in real life, but the instantaneous healing of magical items was still captured well in human games, as the cheese seemed to put the effect over the top and her "HP" so to speak, was restored. Coughing a few times Maux's mother bolted upright and looked panicky around the room, "Where…." but her red orbits went even wider as she saw the two humans standing above her and her mouth opened up for a scream before Maux gripped her in as hard a hug as he'd ever seen the little guy give.

"Welcome back to the land of the living," Ant's mother said, but then gave Ant a look before he realized he'd never made any introductions. "Oh, well, this is my mother, she helped us get the potions needed to bring you back to health…"

"I'm sorry ma, I couldn't save you." Maux interrupted, a pleading in his voice, "The portal-"

"It is alright child," Maux's mother said with a smile exposing a wayward tusk beneath her lip, "It not your fault, I dodge him for many portals before he got me, but my reading not so good enough to…spell better than portals," she continued. Anteros then kicked himself a little more for not figuring that out sooner, though he supposed he couldn't have changed it anyway. They still would have went after her of course, but perhaps not ambushed like they were.

"Like my son said, I'm his mother, Vinalia, and…you are?"

Ant flichned, he'd never even bothered to figure out Maux's mother's name. There was going to be some serious social anxiety flashbacks about this moment in his future. "Wenvan, thank you for help," she replied, "Call me Wen," but though she was clearly greatful the human concept of shaking hands was apparently lost on her as Vinalia just sort of awkwardly ate that pause and moved her hand to her purse.

"We rescued you, but we had nowhere to go but back here. This is where I go to school," Ant said, breaking the silence. "Well, hopefully, if you don't get yourselves killed, how dare you put someone else in danger like this!" Vinalia said, whipping around her famous temper now that the situation was seemingly improved. But then she looked around at Wen and Maux and her expression softened, with a sigh she continued, "I just worry about you kiddo, come here," and she reached over for him to hug her, and he did, but then she undid his pants and he was a little shocked.

"Mom!" Ant said in protest.

"What? I'm still your mother, I think I can change my kid's diaper," Vinalia said as she lead him over to a daybed in the opposite corner of the apartment next to his desktop computer that was currently serving as Ant's changing table. It had a simple sheet covering a waterproof mattress protector of the same type that could be found on Ant's bed, but smaller, this sheet being covered with comic book superheroes. Removing the stuffed bunny and humanoid turtle from their resting places on it, chuckling at the fact that he kept so many of them around, she let Ant lay down on it and began the process of removing his used diaper.

He hadn't pooped(thank the gods he thought) but he was incredibly wet. They were so worried about Wen's health status that he hadn't bothered checking him or Maux since their original change now several hours in the past. Nonetheless she ran a wipe down his backside anyway, and scowled a bit when she brought it up to place it in the pail beside the table. "Bit of film" she said, a side effect of Ant's incontinence, even if he didn't have any solids, there was a constant rate of leakage that his diaper absorbed. She went over to the storage containers holding his supply of diapers and pulled out one of the clothlike ones and as Ant raised up his exposed lower body slightly she placed it beneath him, wiping his front diaper area and applying his nearby rash cream and liberal amount of powder before taping each wing down on him.

"There you go, all better," she said while helping Ant to his feet and giving his diaper a light pat that felt like it turned Ant even redder, if that was even possible. After kicking his pants up into her hands, Vinalia placed them in the hamper Ant had hanging on his door, then handed him a shirt. "But…" Ant started, "Don't worry about it, I know how you like to hang out and I'm fixin to leave," she replied as she pulled the shirt down over his head, his diaper exposed beneath.

"Mama, I-er...thanks." Ant said as he gave her another hug, "Don't mention it," she said wryly before turning her attention to his goblin companions. "I suppose you probably need one too, eh?" Vinalia said looking at Maux's drooping diaper.

Maux turned the deep green goblin equivalent of a human blush, his pants were still in the Azurefel forest. "I'm sorry, ma," Maux said looking back at his mother, still sitting on the bed leaned back against the wall, "But humans have made some innovations I approve of, I have to say," the Goblin said as his mother chuckled and nodded her approval.

Maux hopped down and was helped over to the daybed/changing table by Ant's mother. As she pulled one of the baby diapers out of Ant's containers and began repeating the process she'd done to Ant(himself snickering that Maux had actually pooped), "Reminds me of when Ant was a baby," she said with a smile as she finished taping him up, and gave him a similar pat as she picked him up from the table and offered him to Wen's waiting arms.

"Thank you so much," Wen said earnestly as she cradled her son. "Now," Vinalia said, adopting a more businesslike tone, "What's our next move?"

Next move? Truthfully Anteros was at a bit of a loss as he popped open a can of cherry flavored citrus soda and sat in his computer chair, no longer concerned about his exposed diaper.

"You haven't thought of one, have you?" Vinalia sounded pretty disappointed as she said it, "What am I gonna do with you boyo?" she said as she shook her head. "Fortunately, I thought ahead," she continued, pulling another clear vial out of her purse, this one housing a lurid purple gurgling liquid within its confines. "Bought this along with the health potion from the apothecary on the riverwalk," she continued, "It'll disguise you for a couple of hours. If we ration it out I should be able to get you back down to New Orleans with me..."

Maux looked utterly dejected as he sat at his child's desk at the foot of Ant's bed. There wasn't a lot of room in the apartment, but since most of their freetime was spent either gaming on their PCs, on missions, or at local gaming stores there wasn't a lot of need for more room.

"I'm sorry, but she can't stay here…" Vinalia started. "She is right. I do not belong in your world," Wen said, pushing herself off the bed and embracing Maux, "I go, but I will learn to keep in touch," she said, crying a little, "You in good hands my boy," she finished as she rose and touched Ant on the elbow.

"It's settled then," Vinalia said, "drink a few sips, that should last long enough to get out of Starkville and onto the highway, but be warned, the stomach ache is atrocious."

The Goblin took what was probably more of a human swallow, but it was still manageable. She crumpled to the floor, her raggedy dress slumping like a tent around her as her skin started to go paler and paler, from a yellow green, to yellow, to dead white before recoloring itself into more of a human peach skin. Her bald head grew a wild mangy bright red hair, as her ears shrunk to merely huge human sized, and her eyes turned a more human green, with full irises. If one didn't know any better, she rather looked like a fantasy Dwarf more than a human. It only gave her secondary characteristics, but her size and frame remained very much Goblinoid.

"It oughta be enough to fool any passersby," Vinalia said, as Wen struggled to get up and clutched her stomach. Ant rushed his wastebasket under her as she retched some bile and dry heaved. "Oh my god, I completely forgot, it's worse if you don't eat!" Vinalia called out, running to Ant's fridge. *Must be where I get it from,* Ant thought. Broth apparently didn't count for much in this sort of thing.

"Is all you drink soda!?" Ant laughed at that, "Sorry mama," he said, "I hadn't really expected company," Ant replied dryly.

Eventually she discovered some cheese wedges Ant liked to snack on occasionally and unwrapped them, shoving them in the dwarf looking goblin-human's mouth. "Eat, it'll help," Vinalia said softly as she could.

"Chewing difficult with these tiny teeth…" Wen said through her full mouth as Vinalia chuckled softly. "We should go now," Vinalia said, "I don't think any of us have clothes that'll fit her, and that rag will really look out of place."

It was currently close to midnight so at least most people were indoors at this hour. After gathering up her supplies, Vinalia reached up and gave Ant a big hug, Wen repeating the gesture downward to Maux. "Try to stay safe Kiddo, I don't want the only times I see you anymore is when things are dying," she said into his ear, giving him a kiss on the cheek.

Anteros couldn't quite make out what Wen said to Maux, but it was likely along the same lines. Their goodbyes said, Ant crashed hard on his bed, Maux doing the same right beside him…

Chapter 9

Anteros finally came to around seven or so that morning, Maux still beside him. He felt unnaturally sweaty like he was covered in…he felt around his abdominal area. *Fuck.* They were so dead tired that Ant hadn't even stayed up long enough to change into a night diaper, and the cheaper clothlike simply wasn't up to the task of a full night's protection. That meant urine soaked sheets.

As he began to remove the sheets, Maux roused from his own slumber nearby(his goblin sized bladder ensuring he wasn't nearly the wetter Anteros was). As the two silently engaged in their morning diaper changes for each other, Anteros thought back to his school days at Académie épique. His mother had made certain that he went to a school that he could maintain a connection to his own kind at. It was a private school for not just Olympiads but all manner of what humans would call "fantasy creatures" and descendants of demigods from various pantheons who chose to make their lives in the Earth's realm, this one for those settled in the Garden District of New Orleans. Unfortunately, even amongst the fantastic, some weirdos were weirder than others. Anteros had been the only Cupid in attendance, and as such, was mostly singled out for his diaper usage in the school and was teased mercilessly for it.

Ant never knew whether there were other diaper users in attendance, student privacy was a thing even in their world, and he probably could've remained anonymous himself if he hadn't been convinced by his mother to try out for some extra curriculars. His particular characteristics making him a decent candidate for sports and she wanted him to seize that opportunity. Little did Vinalia know the strategic error she had committed her son to.

Sports meant locker rooms and jocks. Locker rooms meant changing clothes, which meant Ant singled himself out by changing in the stall, and that was like blood in the water for jocks. It wasn't long before they converged on him like sharks, hungry for the weak. It was also his spectacular misfortune to attend when the primary method of bullying on this particular team happened to be the time honored tradition of pantsing. Naturally this resulted in an exposed diaper when they caught him unawares and before long his identity, lineage, and disabilities were the talk of the school. Hello social pariah. Hello stolen diapers. Hello leaks, and hello some of the worst experiences of his life.

Maux was pouring some milk into a bowl of cereal as Ant was gathering clothes to bring with him on his impromptu laundry trip. It wasn't all bad of course, like everything there was always the occasional brightspot. He'd landed with a group of other social pariahs on campus, partaking in the nerdiest things one could do in a school of epic individuals: Human fantasy games and activities. In particular interest to his group back then, was a trading card game where one role played as a wizard, summoning creatures and casting spells to take down the other's life total. Sadly for him though, that was limited merely to lunch and break periods, the school made sure the sports team managed to stay in the same classes together. And as the only one of them that could put two written words together at the same time, Ant was forced to draw attention to himself every day as the chosen reader for every teacher on campus.

Good times, he sighed as he packed the last few items into his clothes basket. "Rough night, eh boss?" Maux said matter of factly, "Can't remember the last time you wet the sheets," he continued, sitting at his child desk and beginning to shovel spoonfuls of sugar coated cornflakes into his mouth. "Yeah, I gotta remember not to pass out before I get my night diaper on," Ant replied equally as dry, Maux chuckling. Anteros wasn't quite sure what to say to him, he blamed himself hard for getting his friend's mother in danger. *What am I even doing?* He thought.

"So, what's our next move?" Maux asked. "That's a good question, one I'm not entirely sure I know the answer to," Ant started, "and I'm not sure I have a right to answer it at all, Maux-" but Maux cut him off, holding up a clawed finger, "We're partners, Boss, so don't mention it," the goblin replied. "Now what's our next move? We must've stumbled on somethin hot for them to go through all that trouble for little ol'us," he continued. Ant deflated, he was still racked with guilt and he'd likely spend the rest of his days trying to make it up to him, but the acceptance of the unspoken apology helped somewhat.

"That's true, I'm just not sure what. We need more intel," Ant said, stating the obvious as Maux drained the bowl of milk. "Fortunately," Maux replied, a devilish grin on his face, "I think I might have somethin useful for that," hopping down from his chair and reaching a hand into his own bed. Anteros' jaw dropped at the sight of what the goblin pulled from it. "I believe you know what this is," Maux said as he held up what looked for all intents and purposes an ordinary thumb drive, but with a tiny golden trident etched onto its side. "Holy shit! How did you...?" Ant spit out as Maux's grin turned to a smirk, "Swiped it off our Cycloptic would be killer as he became just desserts." Ant chuckled at the pun.

Even highly sought after, Mercenaries didn't need the trace gumming up their works. Paper, magical, or otherwise. As such the Cyclops contacts, invoices, and other such red tape of the trade would be housed on the drive. There was a catch though, it wouldn't function on just any computer. The Gods didn't exactly use Windows or even Apple, their OS was proprietary, programmed by Minerva herself, and the Goddess of Wisdom and Strategy wasn't exactly going to leave open doors for hacking either.

"You little devil," Ant said with a grin of his own, "So much for staying safe I guess."

Anteros slipped on some pants and Maux his baby beanie and footed onesie and the two of them made their way to the onsite laundromat for the dorm, the clothes basket on one hip, and gripping Maux's hand with the other. The goblin wasn't much for Pacifiers like his mostly human friend, they simply didn't stand up to the punishment of his fanged mouth. Instead he preferred the much more sturdier teething rings to satisfy his own oral fixation, and he was going to town on one as the two walked down the hallway. In some ways, Ant kind of envied his companion's ability to freely play the part of a toddler, albeit a slightly horrifying one if anybody got too close.

Fortunately nobody was currently using the laundry and Anteros took the opportunity to think over how they would approach this current operation. "Well, we know we can't crack the thing," Maux said through intermittent chewing, stating the obvious but clearly thinking along the same lines. "Yeah, and we can't purchase a compatible computer in this realm, and I don't know about you, but I think I'm all portaled out at the moment," Ant replied. "You said it brother," Maux shook his head.

Anteros crinkled a bit as he shifted position, his diaper rustling across the chair's plastic seat. "Well, maybe we don't need to crack it," Ant said, thinking out loud as

Maux raised a thin mound of skin that passed for Goblinoid eyebrow. "We could hack the old fashioned way…"

"You're stupid, *and* crazy!" Maux said with a laugh. "But maybe just stupid enough to work though…" Ant said as the beginnings of a plan began to form in his head. "You can't possibly think *they're* stupid enough to fall for that, Ant!" Maux continued his protest.

"I can, and I do," Ant replied plainly, "Besides, I don't see you coming up with any better ideas."

Maux sighed, "I'm gonna regret this, but I gotta hand it to yah, you got nerve, Boss…"

Chapter 10

Most people think hacking is typing furiously into a computer where it does all the techno-science-y stuff and spits out the information one wants. Unfortunately, the real thing is…well, not that, *and honestly kind of boring* Anteros thought as he sat in front of his computer, clad in diaper and t-shirt, pacifier tucked firmly in mouth. Any minute now he'd know if his scheme worked. Ant sent it the night before, and the employees oughta be coming into work right about now, 9AM.

On the computer sat a copy of the email he'd sent out:

Dear User,

This is to notify you for the final time that we will have to stop processing incoming emails on your account since you have refused to upgrade your account and we might be forced to lock up your account if this notice is ignored.

Upgrade Now

This restriction will be disabled immediately once we confirm upgrade successful.

Trident IT-Desk

If they clicked the link it would take them to a login page that would merely send their username and password to Ant's own email, one he'd set up right before composing the message strictly for this particular task.

Minerva would have laughed at how obviously fake it was, well, right after she got done smiting Anteros, but all it would take is one sucker among the hapless Daimones to answer the call, so to speak.

Ant realized he'd wet himself right around when the first ping came up on his phone indicating he'd received an email on the burner address.

Glaucus.Neptune@trident.com
Ovidherb

Ant chuckled as he read it, causing a bit more wet to escape into his diaper, the old sea-god was perfect for his little trap. Shifting his pacifier over a bit in his mouth he started to type up phase two when he heard a knock at the door. "Maintenance!" another knock followed, louder this time. *FUCK!!!!*

Ant spit his pacifier out and jumped up as fast as he could, struggling to get into some pants, Maux doing the same to his teething ring as he scampered under the bed in a flash. It felt like an eternity passed but he'd only gotten his pants about halfway over his diaper when he heard the telltale *click* suggesting that Maintenance cared not whether Ant desired company or not and the door swung open.

"Hello we're just gonna…." and the man's voice trailed off as he clearly noticed a slender college student wearing a diaper in front of him, this diaper in particular having a flashy bright space print on it, pants halfway up. The man shook his head, "spray for bugs for a minute," and he began to spritz around the corners of Ant's dormitory room. Ant could clearly see him double take at the pacifier on Ant's table, he hadn't had time to put it in its container and hide it out of sight. It certainly didn't help that he had several stuffies out on his bed and changing table, clearly diapered themselves. *Fuckers didn't put up a notice!* Ant thought.

Normally when maintenance was going to do something like this they put out a notice at least 24 hours in advance and he was able to make the place semi-presentable to normies for a bit. Of course that Ant hadn't been here for long stretches of time meant he could've missed it even if they did.

"Well, uh…have a nice day, um, sir," the maintenance man said, tipping his hat and clearly shaking his head on the way out the door, Ant closing it behind him. "Caught us with our pants down, eh Boss?" a gravelly New Jersey accent called out from under his bed, in between chuckles. "That's not funny," Ant replied as stonefaced as he could, but he couldn't help but let out a little chuckle as he did so. "I just hope they don't decide to come snooping around here more often, it's not a lease violation, but they don't like anything out of the ordinary in here either," Ant continued. "Yeah, wouldn't want mamma and daddy warbucks to be scared off the campus for little johnny, eh?" Maux quipped, leaving Ant to wonder when the Goblin had bothered to watch Annie. "Especially when they're scared off for little johnny by a couple of littles," Ant chuckled with a quip of his own.

With a sigh Ant returned to his seat at his computer, Maux doing the same pulling up his MMO, "Back to the grindstone," he said, inserting pacifier back into mouth and starting to suckle for concentration.

About twenty minutes later Anteros had arranged for his own fake maintenance company to be scheduled for bug spraying in Glaucus' office the following morning. He was an old fart, but as a deity he was high enough rank that nobody questioned an email sent from his address.

"Alright buddy, we're in," Ant said, and Maux gave him a thumbs up before looking up from his game, "I just hope you don't get us both killed in this," the Goblin replied. "You and me both. Now, I think I'm ready for a diaper change…"

Chapter 11

"Well Boss, moment of truth" echoed Maux's voice in his ear.

Anteros was standing outside the front door of Trident Industries, the closest Neptune affiliated office to Starkville, located in scenic Fondren. The building looked as unassuming as could be, a beige warehouse in the middle of an industrial park, and Ant tried to look equally unassuming in the hot Mississippi sun, humidity bearing down upon his beige jumpsuit. He hoped the sweat in his diaper area didn't produce a rash or he'd be quite unhappy. *Why do these guys even wear these things?* He thought as he mustered the confidence to stride purposefully through the door.

Nodding politely at the secretary Ant continued down the narrow hallway as if nothing was out of the ordinary. It was a dimly lit building, mostly black walls, and dark grey carpeting, after the secretary's front desk were a row of cubicles, that Ant made a show of spraying with his bucket of water. The bag carrying his crossbow pistol and rounds, as well as his laptop and the jump drive in question strained against his shoulder as he sprayed around the ubiquitous grey cubicles populating the majority of the building.

At least there's air conditioning, he thought, a lot of air conditioning even, it was quite cold in the building, which was an odd waste of money for what appeared to be a lowly call center. *Gods for you,* Ant thought as he shook his head. "Alright boss, Glaucus' office should be at the end of hallway, it'll be a physical room," Maux piped up in his ear, the camera feed to his own computer back at his dorm being run through the side of his jumpsuit. Glaucus was a higher up, so he wouldn't be in a cubicle like the lesser Daimones who worked the phone lines, clearly the old man had worked his way into a cushy gig as owner of this particular subsidiary. Not bad for someone who started out as human.

Ant heard the story in one of his textbooks in high school, Glaucus had been a sailor in Ancient Greece, before he'd consumed a plant cultivated by Neptune himself that granted him immortality, at the expense of losing his legs and growing a fish tail and fins. Like most of their kind, he could use a spell to give him the appearance of human anatomy, but it was merely an illusion. In doing so, he had become an Olympiad, his bloodline magically connected to Neptune himself.

The story was famous, but mainly because of the magical herb, they usually neglected to mention that Glaucus himself became a miniscule cog in a very large machine. It was in fact surprising to Ant that the old man had been given charge of anything considering the reputation he had as a lowly half breed.

There were comparatively few employees wandering around, due to the nature of the work, most were hunched over in current pursuit of answering phone calls. Ant could hear the occasional call from a boat seeking maintenance, or a worker on an offshore oil drilling platform seeking a pickup or rescue. If you were in trouble out at sea, Glaucus apparently was the man to call.

Arriving at the glass door of a room at the end of the warehouse, Ant confidently strode in, the slight crinkle of his diaper being the only thing to give away the fact that he didn't belong there at all. Sitting his bag on the floor beside the desk, itself covered in various fishing memorabilia, such as hooks, fish statues, and other such novelties, Ant pulled out the thumb drive and got ready to go to work.

"You're an idiot," said a sultry voice behind him and Anteros froze in his tracks, and before he'd even had time to turn around he was shoved against a wall, elbow shoved in his neck, arm held against his back. "Boss!? What's goin on!? Lost video! ANTEROS!!?" but that was the last he'd heard his friend as the earpiece was torn out of his head by his attacker.

The room went so quiet one could hear a pin drop, but much to Ant's chagrin what one actually heard was the unmistakable trickle of Anteros wetting his diaper. "Well, that's one way of confirming it I suppose," the woman said into his ear. "I haven't seen you since Académie épique," she said as she used her leverage to turn him around, still keeping him pinned against the wall. It was at that point he finally got a good look at her, and he instantly knew exactly who she was.

She was a bit heavier than Ant, with round hips, currently covered by a standard Trident uniform consisting of blue collared polo shirt and black trousers. She was about a foot shorter than Ant too, which she fervently used to her advantage, her lower positioning keeping the leverage with her, leaving Ant completely unable to move against the wall as he perused her olive skin, slightly paler than Ant's own, with bright vivid green eyes and dark inky black hair.

"Nereid, it's been too long," Ant finally opined in his best nonchalant voice. "Do you greet all the pest control personnel so warmly, or is this just special for me?"

"Don't try me, Ant," she said with a frown pursing her plump lips, currently colored the same vivid shade of green as her eyes, "and cut the crap, you think checking grandfather's email wasn't the first thing I did when I got here? Now tell me, why are you doing this?"

Ant struggled with how to answer that exactly. Involuntarily his eyes darted towards the thumb drive currently sitting within his palm held against the wall behind him, golden trident clearly visible.

"What the hell?" she abruptly let him go at that point, grabbing hold of the drive. "Where did you get this?" the furious resolve in her voice replaced by one of bright curiosity. It would almost be cute if she hadn't just been about to kill him, in that light it was closer to creepy how fast her demeanor spun on a dime.

Anteros decided to just go for broke, after all, if she was going to actually kill him she could have had fifty Daimones in here by now. "My companion swiped it from the Cyclops when he tried to kill me. Twice," Ant said matter of factly.

"Must have done somethin pretty bad to get him called on you. I hear his services aren't cheap," Nereid responded plainly as she sat at the computer and pushed the drive into the front facing USB port. "You're lucky he turned up dead before he could finish that job, can't believe you somehow got away," she continued. Ant decided discretion was the better part of valor and did not correct that assumption. Though Glaucus had entered the family through magical, rather than the traditional means, the Cyclops was still a cousin to Nereid. Technically a cousin to Anteros as well, but much more distant since he was not descended from Neptune's line.

A list of files appeared on the monitor before Nereid, Anteros moving into position behind the office chair she occupied. Most of them were files on targets, others invoices from carried out orders, but one in particular caught his eye. "That one, there, click on it," he said, pointing at a file that read HOSTILE TAKEOVER, clearly the Cyclops didn't mince words when it came to file names. "Hey, who put you in charge here?" Nereid spat in an annoyed tone, but she nonetheless clicked on the file. And what they saw in front of them sent them both into shock.

It was a memo from Juno, the Queen of the Gods. Technically Anteros' many times great grandmother. In it was a detailed plan to revolt against Jupiter, her husband and King of the Gods. In his place would be put Neptune, Jupiter's brother. As the two of them read on, the final piece of the puzzle was put into place for Anteros, as the Daimones role in this was put into words. They were meant to ensure the earth warmed considerably, allowing for the ice caps to melt and the world's oceans to swallow much of the landmass. Heavily populated land masses. At which point the balance of power would shift, and the Seas would overtake the Skies, now polluted with carbon based greenhouse gases, and Neptune would rise to prominence as King of the Gods, with Juno serving as regent.

Of course, all of the Olympiads were aware of Juno's legendary jealousy with Jupiter's many flirtations and dalliances outside of their marriage. How could she not be? She was the personification of monogamy after all. But, Ant would never think she would go so far as to actually stab Jupiter in the back! The memo ended with some vague promises that the seas would rise and plunge humanity into chaos, in which case they would somehow return to their old ways of worship, providing the place of prominence the Olympiads enjoyed in eons past that would fuel their supposed return to glory.

"This is heavy, Ant," Nereid finally spoke up with some trepidation in her voice. She looked up at him with a raised eyebrow, "You really did uncover somethin pretty bad, didn't you?" she said with some…was it appreciation? Ant's heart involuntarily fluttered a bit at that thought. That was a new feeling he'd have to wrestle with later.

"Yeah, this makes a lot of sense though," Ant blurted out. "What does?" Nereid replied incredulously. "Well, I've been…" Ant struggled with the right word, "Investigating in a sense a lot of Daimon activity lately, one of whom told me he was in New Orleans to keep the drilling going. Now I know why," Ant finished. "That must've been why they sent the Cyclops after you, you were getting too close," Nereid observed. "This is gonna get a lot of people killed Ant, and not just humans, our kind too," Nereid continued, the resolve returning to her voice. Though she was Olympiad, her family's unnatural origins meant that she was much closer to those humans than even diluted Anteros was. A fact that was not lost on their high school classmates, having set her up as a fellow social pariah due to her low status, and ultimately into Ant's gaming group's waiting arms. And a fact that was not lost on Nereid herself as she was concerned for her fellow man, so to speak.

"So I want in, I don't know how you stumbled into this information in the first place exactly, but I want to be a part of tearing it down," Nereid continued. "What? You'd stand against your own family?" Ant said incredulously. "I think you of all people should know how tenuous family can be," Nereid replied dryly, "And even if it wasn't, they look down on us now just as hard as they did in High School."

"Glaucus," Nereid continued, Ant taking note that she was not calling him grandfather at this point, "might be willing to sell out mankind for some scraps of recognition by the Daimones, but I'm not," and she looked him square in the eye with that last sentence, "I want in."

Anteros sighed, "Alright, I hope you know what you're getting into though, it hasn't been an easy haul for me of late, the Cyclops wasn't easy for me to defeat," and he immediately gasped when he'd said it. *Fuck*, he thought.

"You…killed the deadliest assassin of men?" Nereid looked more surprised than anything else. "Well, I'm impressed, I didn't think you had it in you," she said, giving him a wink. Ant gave a deflated sigh, I suppose with the speech against her family it shouldn't have been surprising, but he was afraid for a bit nonetheless.

"Now," Nereid said as she got up from the computer and walked to the door of the office, lowering the blinds so that the outside fluorescents were no longer shining in, and the only light provided was by an incandescent lamp in the corner of the room. "I believe you're quite wet, and someone needs to take care of that for you," she said.

"Wait, are-are you-" but she cut off Ant's protests as she strode over to his bag and pulled out the spare diaper he kept in it, along with his emergency diapering supplies of wipes and travel bottles of his powder and rash cream. "I know you need it, and it's not like I haven't changed a diaper before," she said with a grin, taking hold of his jumpsuit and pulling down the zipper.

Ant followed her motions without resistance, as she laid him down on the floor in front of the desk, now only his diaper covering his otherwise naked body. Very much wet, the little aliens that represented the wetness indicator having long since disappeared.

"Wow, I wouldn't have thought you'd go for the...interesting ones," she said, referring to the ABDL diaper he was currently wearing, as opposed to the medical ones he typically wore when they were in high school. As she pulled back the diaper, it exposed the modified baby diaper currently housed within that served as his booster. "And a full on baby diaper too!" she giggled, and Ant couldn't help a simultaneous feeling of shame and embarrassment, completely entwined with blissful acceptance that he was having his diaper changed by a peer. The feeling was intoxicating.

Nereid placed the fresh diaper under Ant's lower body and removed a wipe from the small container, wiping around his front area, small enough as it was to easily fit within the baby diaper. Then she applied the cream to his rash sensitive areas, Ant silently pointing out where those were, completely consumed in the headspace of the moment. Afterwards she pulled up the front of the diaper and taped it around him, keeping it snug and secured. She was clearly a pro at this.

She patted his padded butt after she helped him from the floor, "The diaper's bigger, but you're a lot more cooperative than the toddlers I'm used to," she said sweetly, and Ant blushed harder than he'd ever blushed before as she helped him into his jumpsuit.

"Um...thank you," Ant said sheepishly. "It's no problem, you needed it," Nereid replied as she pulled up the blinds. "Don't be a stranger now, I want to be in the loop of course," and with that she kissed him lightly on the cheek, placed a card in his hand, and made her own way out of the room.

Ant watched her go with the strangest combination of emotions he'd ever felt in his life. It was only when her swaying gait rounded the corner of the closest cubicle row that Ant shook his head and placed the earpiece back into its rightful place. "ANT!!! Please, answer me buddy!" the Goblin's frightened pleas finally reaching their desired destination. "I'm okay my friend," Ant said dazed, "Better than okay, a lot just happened," Ant continued a bit more put together. "A lot better have! You had me worried sick, I was about to risk a locator spell for your ass!" Maux said, his rage beginning to increase.

"Don't worry man, I'll tell you all about it when I get back. I think I'm in love," Anteros said before muting the mic feed so as to not channel the sounds of him walking out of the building back through the other end.

"What the fuck!?" reverberated through Ant's ear as he calmly exited the door.

Chapter 12

As summer really started to get underway Anteros stayed in constant contact with Nereid. At first through sporadic email, then through PMs over the Agora forums, and finally they had exchanged Discord server information and talked on regular basis.

Ostensibly they were supposed to be talking about the Daimones and their plans for Olympiad domination, but somehow they kept getting off topic. As it turns out Nereid had a deep obsession with the Japanese kids show Super Sentai, which while not as familiar with it per se, was the same show used for footage on Ant's own favorite show, the Power Rangers.

The two would bond over this mutual infatuation as they would spend time over their voice server talking as they watched each other's shows, Nereid getting Ant to watch some Sentai, and Ant getting her to enjoy some Power Rangers. These conversations would naturally reveal other commonalities including a love of Anime, and young adult novels.

It wasn't long before they were playing MMOs together, Nereid's hulking Night Elf Paladin providing the perfect tank compliment to Ant's Goblin Mage DPS(short for Damage Per Second), with Maux's Ranger often accompanying them on raids and dungeon crawls throughout the expansive world.

It was on of these video game adventures that Nereid had mentioned that she was part of a weekly tabletop roleplaying group and invited Ant and Maux to go. Anteros could've jumped for joy when she did, he'd been wracking his brain for neutral location for them to meet to hangout on, and he couldn't come up with anything. Everything seemed too much like a date and though they seemed to really be hitting it off in his mind, he wasn't certain she was looking for a relationship or wanting to take the next step to dating yet.

"I just don't know, Boss," Maux said nonchalantly as he was taping up a fresh diaper onto Anteros. "Aren't you afraid it might be too fast?" the Goblin continued. "What do you mean? We've been hanging out for awhile now..." Ant replied.

"I know, but don't you think it's just a little odd that you meet the girl of your dreams on a mission? Who changes diapers and is super into your favorite show?" Maux questioned, pressing into his argument.

"Well, Sentai and Power Rangers aren't the same..." Ant interjected.

"You know what I mean! What if she's doing all this on purpose? What if this RP thing is a trap!? She's a sea nymph!" Maux blurted out, but he immediately regretted it.

"Oh yeah, because a Goblin is totally trustworthy, right!? Should I judge you that way!?" Anteros retorted, his temper rising.

"I'm sorry, that's not what I-"

"What wasn't what you meant!? You should know better than anyone what prejudice like that causes!" Anteros said, cutting him off.

"I'm just worried 'bout you man!" Maux said with a yell, and the Goblin reached out to hug him, sitting on the changing table Ant was roughly chest height to him.

"I'm sorry, I like her too, but it just feels like we're moving really fast, and we haven't done anything about this hostile takeover since Trident. It's just really…weird." Maux continued, tears welling up around his red goblin eyes.

"I know buddy," Anteros said softly lowering his voice, "and I appreciate it. I'm sorry for getting angry too. Look, we'll stay on alert, I trust her, we go way back, but you're right, if something's too good to be true, it usually isn't. But we still oughta go, if it works out? Great, but if not we'll know she wasn't trustworthy after all."

"Thanks boss, I-" but Anteros cut him off again, "Also, you know, you're invited, you can keep an eye out, it's other Olympiads so non-humans won't be all that unusual. You can keep your eyes peeled for me," Ant said with a smile.

"You can count on me man," the Goblin said with a grin, and Anteros switched places to change Maux's own diaper.

A few minutes later Anteros was dressed in simple black pants, drawstring tied to provide extra support for his diaper, and a shirt featuring the Red Power Ranger emblazoned upon it. Maux in his footed toddler onesie, also featuring a Power Rangers print, though for lols his was the Green Ranger, it also featured a hoodie that would allow him to conceal his ears on the bus ride over.

Slinging his diaper bag upon his back, Ant and Maux made their way down the street to the busstop and it wasn't long before it arrived at its scheduled time. Anteros kept everything in his diaper bag, the side pocket held his wallet, the top pocket several phone cables and an external power bank, the middle pocket travel size diaper rash cream and baby powder, and in the bottom pocket contained a complimentary bag for a bottle of liquor. Ant didn't drink often, both because he was a colossal lightweight, and because it was a diuretic and increased chances of leaks, but the bag didn't contain any liquor, as was popular among his generation, it was perfect for transporting things like trading card games, models, and in this case, a couple of portable gaming consoles.

While sitting on the bus, he pulled the portable games out of the liquor bag and he and Maux spent the short trip playing a grand prix in a kart racer.

It wasn't long before they'd exited the bus and were standing at the front door of another apartment near Ant's college campus, a nondescript brick building not too dissimilar to the one Ant stayed at. Probably even built by the same company from the looks of it. "Better knock I suppose…" Ant said, pantomiming his best C3PO parody. Maux grinned at the joke as Anteros gave the door a light rap.

It was all he could do to keep from throwing his arms around her immediately. Her curvy frame, long black hair, and piercing deep green eyes (this time accompanied with a pair of thick horn rimmed glasses whose frames were a matching green color) being a thing he'd dreamed about more than once, though there was no way he could possibly tell her that. She was wearing a simple pair of jeans, classic green converse, and emblazoned on her t-shirt were the Sailor Scouts of Sailor Moon fame. "Yeah, I'm basically blind without them, but the contacts can get a bit uncomfortable so I don't wear them when I can avoid it," Nereid said as she pushed the glasses up her nose. Ant realized he must have been staring, he uttered a nervous chuckle, before Nereid abruptly saw the Goblin clutching his knee. "And you must be Maux!" she called out brightly.

"Yeah, um…hi!" he said in his gravelly voice, so out of place from how he was currently dressed. "Well come in you two, we're just getting started!" Nereid said as she beckoned them inside.

A group of 4 of them were sitting around a table in the dining room of the apartment, it was arranged in fairly typical fashion, a living room with a TV and several video game consoles, adorned with figurines of various franchises, unlike Anteros' own apartment, this one had a set of stairs leading presumably to a bedroom and bath area. It was fairly nice.

"Alright everybody, these are my friends, Anteros and Maux, Anteros is a cupid," Nereid announced on their arrival, as glowing as ever. "Yo, how's it goin?" a heavy set guy interrupted from the back, he was wheelchair bound, probably wouldn't have looked out of place as a human were it not for his bright red skin and hair that more resembled steel wool than actual hair, in front of him sat a laptop and Dungeon Master's screen. "Um…did you bring a baby?" a taller figure sitting at the table said. This one definitely could not pass for human without an illusory spell, he was covered in thick rocky plate growths. "Ahem," Maux cleared his throat loudly, "I am NOT a baby!" he growled with a flash of anger in his eyes, removing the hood and revealing his long ears and showing his fanged set of teeth, eyes glowing bright in the light of the dining room.

"Oh" the taller figure said with a raised rocky eyebrow, "A Goblin, eh? I didn't think there were any on this plane. Clever disguise I suppose, though you're the smallest Goblin I've ever met!"

Maux took a seat on one of the benched seats surrounding the table with a bit of a "Hmph!"

"He's my friend, I'm Anteros," Ant said, taking his own seat at the table, though much to his chagrin there was a loud crinkle as he did so, and he sat his diaper bag beside him. He had a brief moment of panic as he was no longer certain bringing the diaper bag wasn't a strategic error. It was certainly more convenient, but not everyone was fully aware of what it meant to be a cupid, or were capable of taking him seriously if they did.

Anteros wasn't really sure what to say, he was never very good at smalltalk, and now he was worried about how this whole thing was going to go at all with his diaper bag front and center. A shorter bearded man spoke up at that point, "Have you ever played DnD before?" the voice was pretty shocking as it was a high pitched female voice coming out of a bearded face. Anteros felt a little guilt that he'd misgendered her, clearly she was a Dwarf and he briefly wondered what she was doing on this plane of existence, but he felt the question was too awkward to ask. Especially considering what had just transpired with Maux.

"Um, yeah," Ant stammered as he removed his dice case and sat the diaper bag on the floor behind him. It was originally a hearing aid case that'd been given to him randomly in the French Quarter by a homeless man(Ant had given him a dollar was unable to persuade him to keep it), within was his set of Dungeons and Dragons dice. It was then Anteros noticed Maux struggling with his positioning on the table in front of him as the bench didn't quite offer enough height to rest his arms on it.

"I think I can help with that, I think I've still got my baby brother's booster seat in the closet, my mother left it," the heavyset DM said. With a nod the taller man got up and grabbed a small booster seat out of the closet, helping Maux sit into it. "Your shirt and your onesie are awesome guys, I'm also a big Power Rangers fan," and the DM turned around his laptop to reveal a lockscreen with the morpher from Power Rangers in Space. "Clever," Anteros chuckled, noting that the rangers from that season entered a numerical code for their morphing sequence.

"Alright, so this is meet 0, we're starting character creation today," the DM said behind his screen as Nereid passed out a set of character sheets emblazoned "Pathfinder" in the top right corner, as well as accompanying pencils. "For your stats, you can roll 4 D6s and drop the lowest," the DM continued. Ant grabbed the aforementioned dice from the case and began to roll them as instructed.

Just when he had his numbers written down a rumble occurred in his stomach area, accompanied by Ant's biggest fear at the present time: the unmistakable odor of a messed diaper. Fortunately the diapers themselves contained odor neutralizers that would help to keep it from being too bad, but Nereid was currently sitting right by him on the bench and gave the unmistakable nose wrinkle of someone who smelled a dirty diaper.

Oh fuck, she smells it.
What am I gonna-?
What if she-?
I'll never be able to-

Giving him a furrowed lip, Anteros red in the face as his panicked thoughts flooded his brain, Nereid directed towards him a slight nod. "Don't worry Ant, I'll do it," Nereid said, in a very soft but determined tone. "What is it?" the taller man said from across the table. "Me and Ant will be back," she said matter-of-factly as she picked up his diaper bag from the floor, and Ant's mouth hung open in shock, "No, that's alright, I can-" but he was cut off as she abruptly grabbed his bag, "It's fine," she said, as Anteros looked anxiously around the room. Nobody seemed to care though as they were engrossed with their character creation steps. "Could you grab me a 7up from the fridge on the way back?" the DM said clearly looking at Nereid.

"No problem," Nereid said as she led him to the downstairs bathroom, his diaper bag in tow, Maux almost jumped up, but lodged in the booster seat it was difficult for him to do so, and Anteros shook his head to show him to stand down.

The bathroom was a little cramped, with blue bathroom rugs, a shower with a simple blue curtain, and a towel rack with a couple of blue towels. *Guess they really like blue,* Ant thought as Nereid positioned him in a standing position against the wall. *What in hell am I doing?* He thought, it was one thing for her to change him at Trident, he was only wet then, a diaper he'd messed was a whole different story in his mind. She untaped his diaper, but only pulled down the back, leaving the front positioned to receive any liquid in case Ant wet himself mid change. The smell made him the height of embarrassed, "I'm sorry, you don't have t-"

"It's okay" she said a little shaky but clearly determined, "It's not a problem, if I didn't want to do it I wouldn't have dragged you back here."

With that she removed a wipe from the container housed within his diaper bag and began removing poop and placing the used wipes in the cupped diaper. Anteros was held against the wall as she did so, "I'm sorry…"

"Please quit saying sorry," Nereid replied, a note of pleading desperation in her voice, as she concentrated on what she was doing. Slowly the wipes began penetrating deeper in his butt and Anteros involuntarily shuddered a bit, as he was wont to do when fingers worked their way over his anal area. Anteros stayed quiet though, he didn't know what he'd do if she got any on her hand or worse, had to clean any off the floor. As the final wipe was placed in the used diaper, and she removed it from him, she silently directed he turn around, but was a bit apprehensive as to what to do with the messy one (It was quite a bit larger than the baby diapers she was used to) but in the end awkwardly taped it up so all of the mess was contained within the diaper just as she would have one of them.

Removing a final wipe she wiped down his front and applied some of his rash cream and powder to the places he'd pointed out to her the last time. Taking a diaper out of his bag, Ant grabbed one end with his hand and held it in place against the wall as he breathed a sigh of relief that she hadn't seemed to get any of his accident on anything or herself. Nereid then removed a modified baby diaper from his bag, raising an eyebrow. "Yeah, um," Anteros struggled for a minute with how to word this exactly, "you place it between the leak guards and it's a booster for me," he said as plainly as he could given the circumstances. "Explains the one at Trident then, I have to admit, I was a bit perplexed there," she said as the baby booster was placed inside the larger diaper and pulled the front up into his crotch, and taped him up, patting the butt of his diaper as she helped him back into his pants.

She found the supply of plastic grocery bags he kept in the side pocket of his diaper bag, and deposited his used diaper within one, both of them seemed to want to say something but no sound came out as Anteros took the bag and tied the ends together enclosing his discarded soiled garment within. "Um, thanks-It's no problem" both of them at the same time and chuckled awkwardly as the air felt like it was sucked out of the room. "Let's get back to the game," Nereid finally said, cutting the tension somewhat.

The stares bore holes into Anteros body as he walked the bag containing his own used diaper into the dining room in front of the whole gaming group before heading out into the front yard to the large bin. (His awkward shuffling actually caused him to miss the miffed grimace on the DM's face when Nereid forgot his soda) What normally would have been absolutely mortifying for him though, enough for him to abruptly leave the party even, was all the sudden a bit more bearable knowing that Nereid seemingly wasn't scared off at the prospect of changing a messy diaper. He still didn't like it, but he would definitely return to the room. For Anteros it was something of a final hurdle, he definitely wanted to pursue her fancy if at all possible. The latter part being a big if for someone as hard to even hold a conversation with, let alone get to know as Ant was.

The meet progressed rather quickly after that, Maux had taken the liberty of finishing the parent values of Anteros' character stats. Ant decided on a half orc paladin he called Grukk, Maux was a half-elf druid, Nereid a merfolk mage(a sly smile at the irony across her face), the tall man a gnomish thief, and the bearded girl a half-elf barbarian. The races were obviously fantastic to humans, but they were either commonplace or hysterically inaccurate to those who travelled between worlds. That was part of the fun, but also why it was only the nerdiest of the nerd that engaged in it among their kind.

As they were getting up to leave, however, Anteros received a text message from Nereid informing him to wait out front for her. They needed to talk.

Anteros and Maux were directed to Nereid's car, she had offered to give them a ride rather than having to take the bus back so they could talk. She drove a 1995 Geo Tracker, conveniently with a carseat, "For my nephew", she said as Maux was secured within it.

"I hope I wasn't too forward with you Ant, you just-" Nereid opened up. Anteros was nervous as hell, his heart pounding to escape from his chest. "No, it's alright," Ant finally piped up, "I needed it," he said with the best smirk he could muster, echoing her words from Trident. In the rearview Ant could see Maux with a shocked expression on his face. Nereid grinned, "Good, because I'm gonna be honest-"

"I like you," Anteros blurted the words out before he actually processed them. *This is the end*, he thought. He'd fucked up, she'll never be comfortable around him again, unless she says....?

"What?" Nereid's eyebrows scrunched, "I mean, I like hanging out with you too, Ant. These last few weeks have been great..."

"I'm sorry, I-"

"It's alright, it's just we haven't done anything about the Hostile Takeover! I love watching Sentai and Power Rangers and whatever, but this is so much bigger than that! People are gonna die and we've been just dicking around!" her words were like white hot barbs going directly into Ant's soul. She was right of course, he'd been so focused on his own loneliness, over the prospect of finally connecting with someone of the opposite sex, that he'd lost sight of the mission.
"I'm sorry, you're right, I've-" He stammered as he struggled to find the words, "I need to get focused, I just don't know what to focus on!" Anteros said, getting somewhat defensive nonetheless, as it was the truth, he didn't know what their next move should be.

"Fortunately, I think I can help us there," Nereid replied, smoothly deflecting Ant's defensiveness, "I don't know how much you've been researching, but I've been trying to use Glaucus connections to get an in," she was briefly interrupted by a series of potholes drowning out all sound. Starkville wasn't exactly the most well paved of towns.

"What I've managed to find out is that the Daimones are trying to get one of their own nominated for the United States Congress. They're holding a fundraiser for him, but that's not the important part. Jupiter and Juno are going to be attending this fundraiser personally. This is our chance to expose the plot!"

Nereid had a mile wide grin on her face as she was clearly proud of her actions in this regard, and Ant was fairly impressed himself. "I'll text you the address," she said and though Anteros was somewhat heartbroken at his being rebuffed, he still couldn't quite get rid of a thought from the back of his mind, *It wasn't actually a 'No'.*

"I'll talk to you later kiddo," she said softly as they finally pulled into Ant's apartment complex and he opened the door. *Nobody calls me Kiddo but...*Anteros decided he enjoyed it anyway as he helped Maux out of his carseat and the two of them walked into his apartment.

"Later," he said as the mini-SUV reversed and drove away

Chapter 13

Anteros was a little cramped in the gas station bathroom as Nereid pulled up his dress pants over his exposed diaper. "You look cute," she said with a smile, she herself wearing a green sequined dress the perfect shade of her eyes, and black flats that matched her deep inky black hair. Ant was in a matching shade of green Polo shirt and dress pants, and a black pair of converse. They looked the part of a happy couple. *And I guess we are, or at least will be,* he hoped.

The fundraiser was for a contested Mississippi Senate seat, the Daimones were probably concentrating their efforts in the Gulf South due to how highly intertwined their economy was with oil drilling and exploration, figuring their explicitly pro-fossil-fuel stance played better as such. Despite his general apathy for human politics, the topic did occasionally come up at his human University, so Ant was aware that Mississippi was a reliably red, or Republican, state and that allowed for some guarantee of victory should the Daimones actually get the nomination. It was being held in a private ballroom of the Belle Côte Hotel and Casino in Biloxi along the Mississippi Gulf Coast.

Nereid had gotten the two of them and their "toddler" Maux invites through her connections to Glaucus, allowing them access to the presentation. Only they had no intention of actually watching said presentation as they exited the Geo Tracker and Nereid gave her keys to the valet(naturally, their expenses would be paid for by Trident Industries) and the three of them entered into the expansive entrance way of "the Belle", as the locals called it.

The building was massive, the tallest in the state. Though having grown up in New Orleans it wasn't nearly as tall as the buildings Ant was used to it was certainly the widest building he'd ever seen of the height. It spread out with two secondary wings attached to the main casino area featuring hundreds of hotel rooms. Biloxi was a tourist town, known primarily for its gambling, becoming in recent years one of the primary destinations outside of Las Vegas and Atlantic City for the humans to practice their monetary pastime.

The walls were nearly ubiquitously painted gold, and there was(though both Ant and Nereid chuckled when they saw it) an imitation greek fountain with gray stone statues spouting the water in the middle of the entryway. Olympus was actually very brightly colored with gaudy paint as had the Ancient Greeks preferred to decorate their temples and monuments, but for some reason Humans had mistaken the weather worn grey of their current monuments to be the norm in the era, and it was that they attempted to recreate. Despite this, Anteros figured the gold to be a bit monotone and found a distaste for it for the most part.

Humans were bustling all over, some entering the several shops that lined the first floor of the casino, others making their way to the many slot machines and card tables that adorned the gaming floors. Anteros, Nereid, and Maux were actually after the elevator towards the back of those gaming floors, Maux sticking close to Anteros so as not to be seen among the flashing lights and spinning reels and boisterous dealers scattered about requiring them to occasionally make room for occupants and cocktail waitresses with heavy drink trays.

Nevertheless they were able to hit the elevator and onto the second floor which was a bit quieter with several different amphitheaters and conference rooms currently unoccupied as the floor had been rented out by the Daimones for the ballroom at the end.

"Excuse me," a woman with a deep southern drawl said as their party stopped at the entrance to the ballroom, "But are you on the guest list for this evening?" her quizzical eyebrow suggested she did not in fact believe they were.

"Yes, if you check your notepad I believe you'll find Nereid Naiad, a plus one, and a child's ticket," Nereid replied brightly, and Ant could tell she put as much haughty confidence in it as she could. As the southern woman checked her notepad her eyes widened a bit, she must have been surprised to see they actually were on the list.

She whispered into a small mic attached to her usher's uniform, and directed the two of them inside. The ballroom was a similar gold in color, with a hardwood floor, a massive golden chandelier, and several tables arranged at odd intervals throughout the room. It reminded Anteros somewhat of an awards show like the Tonys or the Oscars as everything was set up to watch their reigning celebrities. Everything was going smoothly so far and Ant was on the top of the world. Nereid was gorgeous in her dress, and he was on what, though for a myriad of reasons beyond their sabotage plans was pretty far from it, could nonetheless be called a pretty wonderful date in his own mind.

An older waiter with pale skin and white hair intercepted them on their way into the expansive ballroom, "If you'll excuse me, Master and Missus," Ant blushed a little at them being referred to as such, "but a table has been prepared for your arrival," and the man ushered them forward towards the table. Smack! Anteros felt a sharp pain in his back as he was abruptly hit from behind and his hands suddenly bound in handcuffs and as he looked up to scream for Nereid a man's hand went for his face, "HAAW!" was all he got out before any further pleas were muffled by the rough hands holding him back. Nereid got similar treatment only barely moving her mouth before a hand grabbed her from behind, a third grabbing Maux who attempted to bite at the man, even drawing blood with his razor sharp teeth before being subdued.

Why!? Was all Anteros could think before he passed out and was dragged out of the building.

...

"What the fuck is wrong with you!? I told Ant it was a trap! I fucking knew it!"

"Stop, Maux, please..."

"No, you don't get to 'please' me, I KNEW IT!"

"MAUX! If I was in on this, then why am I in here too!?"

Here was a barred room of what appeared to be some sort of warehouse, a row of fluorescent lights running the length of the hallway lined with other such rooms. Were it not for the lack of prisoners, and the very much abundance of boxes within those rooms, she could've sworn they'd been interred within an actual prison. Nereid felt awful, she'd gotten them into this mess and at the moment she wasn't sure she'd be able to get them out of it. All her life she'd struggled, caught between the rock of the reputation her family possessed, and the hard place of the fact that she was not much of a sailor like her family wanted her to be. She was always caught between failing the demands of the Glaucus line, and failing to meet the class demands of the other Godlines who considered hers inferior.

Somehow she'd always come through though, but she wasn't so certain she could this time.

"Well then what in the Gods' Names happened out there tonight!?" the little Goblin, somewhat comical to her as he was still in his little tuxedo onesie, angrily shouted back at her.

"I don't know, somehow they knew what we were planning," Nereid responded, of course they would know she was coming, she'd RSVPed, *but how did they know it was for malicious intent?* She wondered. "Yeah, I think I figured that much out for myself, princess," Maux said, clearly still agitated. Nereid rolled her eyes at the 'princess' remark.

"They must have figured you were mine," Nereid said as she began piecing together some thoughts. "Yours?" Maux raised his goblin brow inquisitively. "My baby, that's why we're in here together," Nereid continued, as Maux looked down at his onesie and rolled his own eyes at that point. "Which means they weren't given detailed descriptions of you two, they were clearly after me," Nereid reasoned. *It was my fault*, she thought as a pit began to grow in her stomach.

"Which means you've got a leak," Maux said, chuckling at his own choice of words. The Goblin then sat crosslegged in the middle of the floor and began to chant in a low chorus, *"Ya a khetsaram kiranann du…"*

"What are you doing?"

"Ya a khetsaram kiranann du…Ya a khetsaram kiranann du….Ya a khetsaram kiranann du…."

A muffled POP! Sounded within the room as a diaper bag sprang into existence in front of Maux. "Not all magic is Olympian," Maux said simply as he revealed the small green coin fastened to the stroller attachment on the bag which contained the phrase 'Ya a khetsaram kiranann du' in etched scratchy letters. "One of the trinkets Ant picked up in Azoran," Maux began to explain, "It's the big city in the realm where I'm from, where we met actually. It's a charm with a spell etched into it, created by what passes for human in that plane of existence. It does one thing, makes sure you and a single object it's attached to are inseparable."

"And you never know when or where you're gonna be when you desperately need your diaper bag," Maux finished with a fang-filled smile.

"I didn't think Goblins were capable of magic," Nereid declared, and Maux flared up again, "I'm not like other Goblins…." he said through bared teeth. "Now, I think we at least know you're good for changing a diaper," Maux said, clearly wanting to move on from the subject as he pulled an unmodified baby diaper out of the center pocket.

"Yeah, I think I can do that," Nereid responded, somewhat muted after clearly offending the greenskin. Undoing the buttons at the crotch area of the tuxedo onesie, Nereid removed the soiled diaper from beneath the goblin and proceeded to wipe his bottom, there was a bit of poop there but not enough to really cause a problem for her, changing Maux was not unlike that of some of her babysitting jobs or her nephew really. She really didn't quite enjoy the process per se, of course, but she did like the motherly feeling it gave her to do the deed. Internally she was grappling with the fact that she felt even more strongly in that vein towards Anteros when she changed him, though she couldn't quite figure out how to word it exactly. Just being open to changing someone was one thing, actually wanting to do it in…*that way* was just a too weird something else in her mind.

She gave his bottom a light pat after she taped on his new diaper and rebuttoned his onesie, Maux frowning somewhat as she did, "There, all better," she said as sweetly as she could given the circumstances, ignoring the grumpiness it caused the goblin.

"Now, it won't be long before they realize that trace didn't come from whatever boss this place has," Maux said as he again began to chant, this time in an ancient Olympian that was more familiar to her ears.

The temperature in the room plummeted hard, Nereid found herself shivering as ice began to form around the bars currently holding them in. She gave a silent thanks that she was wearing her contacts, as her glasses probably would have been too fogged to see at this point. Out of the Goblin's hands jets of ice shot directly into her hands, and in them formed a solid ice trident, it was cold, but not too cold to touch, and a hardness that suggested the equal of any trident she'd come across. And into her other hand grew a net made of strung together icicles. She looked for all intents and purposes, save for her gender, the perfect Retiarius

"I presume you know your way around a trident and net, given your family," Maux said matter of factly.

"You would presume wrong," Nereid responded, equally as matter of factly, "I'm fairly terrible with them actually," looking back around at Maux.

"I'm not like other sea nymphs," she said, with mock baring of teeth.

"My apologies," Maux said, another stream of ice hitting her hands, this time transforming the ice-trident within into a massive broadsword and congealing the net into a buckler shield. Not unlike that of her Night-Elf Paladin she played in their MMO, though her sequined gown gave her more of the look of an ancient statue of Minerva herself. "Looks like we both have prejudices we need to work on," the goblin continued as a fiery sledgehammer smashed through their captive bars, bringing any and all further banter to an abruptly hot end.

Nereid raised her buckler to block the flames as shards of metal flew all around her. Surprisingly the ice held as if it was made with the finest steel, but its cool icy exterior kept her from nary a burn as the large red ogre in security uniform raised his hammer above his head for another blow.

A bolt of ice hit the ogre square in the forehead as Nereid took the opportunity to run her broadsword clean through its chest, icicles forming around the open wound as the ogre fell to the floor from her blade.

"Um..." Maux stammered, holding his mouth in disgust. He looked about ready to convulse.

"Look, it's self defense, we'll talk about it later," Nereid said flatly, to which the Goblin nodded solemnly.

"Alright," Maux said, regaining his composure, "I can't do too many more of those bolts if I'm gonna keep your sword and shield intact," he continued, eyes glowing an unearthly red compared to the whites of the fluorescents.

"You need me to be your Tank," Nereid responded with a grin.

"Something like that," the goblin chuckled.

"Alright, let's find Anteros."

...

Gods I'm stupid, Ant thought. Maux had been right all along, she was playing him for a fool. And Anteros had fallen for it, hook, line, and sinker. He might have laughed at the play on words considering Nereid's origins if he wasn't feeling so utterly betrayed. *It was my fault,* he thought as a pit began to grow in his stomach. Thanks to his selfishness Maux was gone or worse...Ant didn't even want to consider what the 'or worse' meant.

Anteros was sitting in an empty room, save for a nondescript metal table, a harsh fluorescent light, his own handcuffs, and the hard metal chair Ant was currently sitting in. The chair made it all the more obvious his diaper was full to bursting as he squished with each movement and struggled to get comfortable. Maux wasn't here to summon his diaper bag of course, and Anteros worried he might never see his companion again.

The single door opened at the far side of the room, interrupting his gloomy train of thought, and into the room stepped a gigantic red ogre. This one was clearly older as his thick kinky hair was starting to grey, and his fangs protruding from his lower jaw touched either end of a bushy salt-and-pepper mustache which seemed to compliment his square framed glasses and dress shirt, tie, and pants combo.

"It must just really tear you up that your girlfriend was workin for us the whole time, eh?" the Ogre said as he placed a file on the table in front of Ant, clearly intent on breaking his spirit further.

But there was something...*off* about the way he said it. Ant couldn't quite put his finger on it, but there was a definite tingling in the back of his head. "You're lying," Anteros replied as his despair receded and was replaced by a renewed flutter in his chest. And a determination that he was going to get out of here.

"Am I?" the Ogre nonchalantly continued, but the tingling only grew stronger in the back of Anteros' mind. One of the abilities Ant was blessed with of course, in addition to his perfect aim and capability to do magic, was an uncanny skill when determining whether someone was lying, as it made the Cupids more able to tell when a relationship was or wasn't working.

"You can't fool me, I'm a Cupid, remember?" Ant continued with a grin, not even caring to notice the growing wet spot on his dress pants as his diaper began to leak; urine trickling down the legs of the metal chair and onto the floor.

A claxon sounded in the distance as a red light began to flash in the gap between the floor and the door. Reaching up to an earpiece in his pointy ear, the older Ogre had a look of horror spread across his face. "A breach? I'm on it!" and the Ogre abruptly sprinted out of the room, not realizing he'd slammed the door so hard it failed to stay shut and bounced open, revealing a brightly fluorescent lit hallway punctuated at intermittent intervals with a regularly flashing red light.

Another thing the Ogre failed to realize is that he left the file on the table. The file currently held together with a simple metal paperclip. Reaching out for the clip, Ant made short work bending it into the proper shape needed to lever the bars inside the rudimentary handcuff locks and before long his hands were free and he sprinted as well as he could himself out of the open door, his saturated diaper forcing it to be more of a fast waddle, even for one as athletically gifted as himself.

The hallway was full of various storage rooms and not really good for sneaking or hiding, so Anteros lost all pretense of it as he tried to waddle down it as best as he could, a trail of urine following behind him with each squishy step until he came face to face with a much younger and much angrier gigantic red ogre, a flaming hot sledgehammer raised over his head.

Anteros had nothing, no time to cast a spell, no crossbow to shoot a bolt from, nothing. This was the end, he was going to die as the Ogre ratched up the flames ready to bring them crashing down upon the hapless Cupid cowering before him, literally wetting himself at the sight.

A fleshy *schlick* sounded as a blade protruded from the Ogre's stomach and he lurched forward, falling flat in front of Anteros with a solid THUD revealing a figure hidden by a buckler and a small, green, tuxedo onesie clad Goblin standing behind the figure, eyes glowing an unnaturally bright red.

"Buddy I am so glad to see you!" Anteros cried out as he reached down to hug his friend, squeezing him hard despite the fact that this caused yet more liquid to squeeze from Ant's diaper.

"I'm happy to see you too Boss, but we gotta go," the Goblin said muffled against Ant's shoulder. At this point the figure lowered its icy buckler from its face and revealed the unmistakable curves of a slightly sweaty Nereid hidden behind its features.

"Ant, I can explain, it's not what you-"

But Anteros cut her off, for the first time in knowing each other, completely confident in what he was about to say, "I know, and it's okay, let's just get out of here," Ant said calmly.

"But how did you figure it out?" Nereid replied curiously. "What's with the tone of surprise?" Ant quipped, but he then pointed at the Ogre currently residing on the ground, "Let's just say one of our friends here let it slip unintentionally," Anteros explained.

"Alright you two, you can flirt later, we gotta go!" Maux griped, causing both Ant and Nereid to blush pretty hard. "Right, I think I've figured out we're in some sort of modified self storage," Nereid responded, her awkwardness immediately replaced with a calm command of the situation. "That means if we follow this hallway through to the end we should find some sort of exit I would think," she finished as Ant and Maux nodded their approval.

With each passing storage door they became more and more anxious that another Ogre was round the corner, but much to their surprise they found the way surprisingly free of obstacles as the bright red exit sign shown in the distance. Just as they themselves rounded the corner of the last row of storage units and came into sight of the exit sign they stopped dead in their tracks.

Blocking it was the older Ogre, another gigantic Ogre, and between their flanks was a sight that sent shockwaves at all three of their faces. A heavy set, wheelchair bound, bright red skinned, steel wool haired, apparent Ogre sat between the two. Their DM had caught them in a trap.

"Imagine my surprise when the pants shitting Cupid that sat at my RP table just so happened to be the very same pants shitting Cupid that killed the Cyclops," the Ogre said in a cocky tone.

"How DARE you talk to him like-"

But Nereid's defense was cut short as the anger flared hard within the Ogre as flames erupted from his wide nostrils, "You shut your mouth, whore!" the Ogre snapped, "I can't believe you would DARE do this to me!" he said, mocking her own words. "I was nice to you! Do you have any idea what being around godstrash like you does to my reputation? But I put up with it, I did it for YOU! You should be honored for that! And you gave me NOTHING!"

"Hey, she doesn't owe you anything man!" Ant spoke up, attempting a defense of his own.

"You shut up too pants pissing piece of shit! Did you even bother to learn my name?" the Ogre said defiantly. And it occurred to Ant that he hadn't really ever bothered to ask any of their names. He was too busy being focused on his own problems at the time.

"This kind of bullshit is why I can't seem to get laid man, there's just no respect for your betters," the Ogre shook his head, "Your corpses won't sell for as much with the Daimones, but it'll have to do. Kill em boys," he commanded to his flanking associates, raising his hand as a signal, who lifted their sledgehammers high over their heads in preparation for an attack.

"No, Erichthonius," Nereid said with a smile as she raised her own buckler in kind, "the reason you can't get laid, is because you're not a nice person. Anteros might still be in diapers, but you're an arrogant, entitled, little child!" and with that she let her buckler fly, spinning so hard it sliced Erichthonius' head clean off his body, black bloodsplatter coating the two ogres beside him, causing just enough hesitation that one received an icebolt straight at his face from Maux, and the other received a skewering from Nereid's icy broadsword. Anteros, thinking quick on his feet, unhooked the set of keys attached to the older Ogre as he fell to the ground, a pool of his own black blood gathering beneath his torso.

The three of them ran out the door of the self storage, a neon sign out front reading, "King of Athens Self Storage" in bold lettering, overlooking a parking lot filled with several cars. It was pitch black out, "Any idea which of these might go to one of those keys, Boss?" Maux said as he surveyed the parking lot of cars.

Anteros raising the keys to his face so he could examine them in the moonlight noticed a keychain emblazoned in big red letters, 'JEEP'. "Yeah, I think I might know the one," Ant replied, as he waddled his way towards a classic open topped Jeep Wrangler parked beneath the neon sign.

It was grey-green in color, but it looked jet black against the night sky as the three of them hopped in, Maux awkwardly buckling a way too large for him seatbelt in the passenger seat, Anteros at first moved to sit in the driver's seat but balked when he saw the manual transmission staring at him in the face, "Um, either of you know how to drive stick?" he inquired.

"Move over kiddo," Nereid said taking his keys, as Ant awkwardly with a swollen diaper between his legs stepped into the backseat, "I got you covered," Nereid said as she cranked the Jeep and revved the engine. The old-school GPS attached to the dash(clearly the old Ogre didn't update with the times) showed they were currently located in Long Beach, MS. About a half hour's drive back to the Belle Côte in Biloxi.

"Not a bad bit of rescuing, huh? You know, sometimes I amaze even myself," Maux chuckled at his own mock impression of Han Solo. "That doesn't sound too hard," Ant quipped back, playing the part of Princess Leia.

But the laughs quickly died as a fireball hurdled past the Jeep as it sped east on the highway towards their destination. "Fuck! This is why I kill them!" Nereid shouted as Maux cringed a little.

Anteros looked back behind them, a silhouette of a sports car shown against the reflection of the Gulf of Mexico, its beach brightly lit by the high moon in the sky. Fumbling around for anything to hurl back at their pursuer in the backseat, Anteros discovered strapped to the bottom of the seat an M1911 semi-automatic pistol with a couple of attached clips. Normally Anteros shared Maux's distaste for killing, it was one of the reasons he preferred arrows to bullets, but in this particular instance? Nereid was right, that cat seemed to be out of the bag. *Besides, beggars can't be choosers,* Ant thought grimly.

Loading up a clip into the pistol, Ant took aim at the car as another fireball hurled past them causing Nereid to swerve the Jeep hard to the left to avoid getting singed. Ant fired a shot off, but it was a rare miss for him, a combination of the rapidly zagging Jeep, as well as his inability to take a proper stance due to his swollen diaper.

Ant made the snap decision that he wasn't going to be able to shoot properly with the wet diaper between his legs. "Gimme a fresh diaper buddy!" Ant yelled out.

"NOW!? Really!? Are you insane!?" the goblin cried out, but grabbing the diaper bag from the floorboard between his legs, Maux handed Anteros a fresh diaper as commanded.

Anteros doing his damndest to maintain his balance as the car sped past and zigged to avoid oncoming fireballs he awkwardly removed his sopping wet pants. *Nereid really knows how to drive, odd trait for a sea nymph,* Ant thought as he untaped the wet diaper. There wasn't time to bother with wipes, creams, or powder, so he simply tossed the wet diaper into the unoccupied floorboard beside him, and attempted to wedge the fresh diaper between his butt and the passenger seat as he stood in the open topped Jeep. No easy feat considering the wind whipping all around him.

Finally he managed to pull the front of the fresh diaper up between his legs as his pants caught an updraft and went flying out of the backseat. "Boss, could you hurry up? He's gaining!" Maux cried out as yet another fireball flew overhead.

Taping up the last tape, clad in nothing but his polo shirt and diaper at this point, Anteros grabbed hold of the M1911. Now able to steady himself he peered down the sights, Godly aim allowing for perfect placement at the end of his arm as he squeezed the trigger, a resounding PSHCHOUWT! Screaming out of the end of the barrel as the bullet crashed through the windshield of the pursuing vehicle and struck its driver square through his eyeball, killing him instantly and causing him to crash over the concrete boardwalk and out into the sand of the beach.

"Nice shot, Ant!" Nereid called out as Anteros finally let his shoulders sag, diaper crinkled against the seat, and breathed a sigh of relief.

"Thanks Nereid," he replied before passing out in the backseat of the Jeep.

Chapter 14

Nereid sighed as she took her Night Elf into the cavernous dungeon along with the accompanying Werewolf character played by her friend. The dungeon looked like a classical lava filled grotto with red rocks and stalactites hanging from the ceiling. At its entrance stood three large green skinned Orcs who ushered in the first quests in the dungeon crawl. It was a low-level dungeon, not even really worth running for characters at max level like hers and her friend's, but they were farming a particular item that was at its highest drop percentage from a flaming hellhound located within. After the ordeal she and Anteros had gone through at the self storage, she felt like she really needed some simple video games in her own home.

"I just don't know what I'm gonna do Sindri," Nereid said into her metallic blue headset mic as she began the process of slaughtering dozens of hellhounds in the name of loot. Nereid was wearing a pair of pajama pants emblazoned with random halloween pumpkins(out of place in the summer, but she didn't really care) and a shirt featuring a giant golden ape surrounded by flame like power from one of her favorite animes. "Do about what, boo?" the high pitched squeaky voice sounded within her ear. The bearded dwarf was the girliest person Nereid had ever met, had she been next to Nereid, rather than across town speaking over Discord, she would've been decked out in Sailor Moon and other Shojo manga gear, and her headset was bright pink and Hello Kitty themed. It wasn't Nereid's style exactly(she was more of a Shonen and Tokusatsu girl after all) but after what had transpired at the King of Athen's Self Storage and the death of Erichthonius, Nereid felt like she could really use some of her bubbly personality.

Sindri had taken the ogre's death pretty well, she'd never really liked him anyway due to his abrasive macho personality and unbearably competitive nature. Sindri barely tolerated Erichthonius purely because he'd been hanging with the group so long and she felt like it would make him even worse if his only friends all of a sudden dropped him. *Now I suppose the dropping took care of itself,* Nereid thought as her character shot some arrows into an enemy Orc, this one dressed in red spikes to contrast the blue ones at the entrance to the grotto.

"I don't know how to expose the Hostile Takeover," Nereid replied as the next room in the dungeon crawl had several Orcish sorcerers casting a spell that empowered a gigantic lava dwelling worm. Were it not for the jagged edges, it would've looked not unlike the sandworms of *Beetlejuice* fame. "I could just broadcast it all over the place, but I don't wanna start a war either," she continued with a frown as she began systematically taking down the sorcerers before turning her attentions towards the worm itself, Sindri's Werewolf following suit.

"Jupiter so rarely leaves Olympus, the Belle Côte was our only hope," Nereid would've almost chuckled at sounding like Princess Leia if depression hadn't been slowly starting to set in.

"Well, I don't want a war either," Sindri said, as matter-of-factly as can be. Sindri was one of the only people Nereid had entrusted with the information, though she served a different pantheon than Nereid's own, the dwarf was still one of her oldest friends. And since the ogres were seemingly after Nereid herself and knew nothing about the conspiracy, she figured her actual mistake had been in telling the gaming group about the ball, rather than informing Sindri of the plot. "A shift in the balance of power probably means Thor rallies the Valkyries and Asgard invades this plane of reality," Sindri explained, an astute observation Nereid probably should've realized herself.

"What if you just went to Olympus and told them?" Sindri inquired. "One does not simply walk into Olympus," Nereid responded in her best Sean Bean impression. "Right, I always forget you Olympiads don't have a--" but Sindri abruptly stopped, "The Bifrost! That's it!" Sindri exclaimed.

"I'm afraid I don't follow," Nereid responded as Sindri's Werewolf took down the last few healthpoints of the Lava Worm. "The Bifrost is what connects my people to this plane of reality," Sindri began. "Yeah," Nereid responded, still not quite on board. "But it doesn't just connect Asgard to Midgard-er-Earth," she said, using her people's name for this realm. "It connects via Heimdall's magic to *every* plane of reality," Sindri's smirk almost being audible across the chat as Nereid finally figured out where all this was going. "But how do we get him to send us to Olympus?" Nereid asked with genuine curiosity. "Well, Heimdall doesn't administer it personally, he's busy drinking mead and keeping watch for Ragnarok," Sindri explained, "My mother works in the Bifrost office, she can patch us through to Olympus," she finished as the large flaming hellhound burst forth from the dead Lava Worm's gullet, the prize for their journey.

Nereid noted the 'us' in that statement, and grimaced at the idea of letting yet another person in on the plot, but figured if Sindri was trustworthy her mother probably was too. She hoped anyway. "How are you gonna convince her to do that?" Nereid countered as they began hitting the flaming hellhound with everything they had, arrows and slashes descending upon the videogame animal. "Do you think she wants her only daughter stuck in the biggest warzone since Jotunheim? She'll want to avoid this as much as we do," Sindri replied solemnly.

The Hellhound exploded into hundreds of tiny magma shards and the two characters received their rewards for the quest. Nereid offered silent prayers to RNGesus, chuckling at the human religion based joke, that she would be blessed with the item they entered the dungeon for. "Well, I guess that's settled then," Nereid said. "Right, you gather the party, I'll make the arrangements, meet me at the metalworking building on campus," Sindri said as their loot appeared before them.

Nereid received a sword she had no intentions of using but was at least worth a dozen gold, and miraculously the item she was looking for: Barbaric Woollies. A seemingly pointless garment offering nothing stats, but she needed to send it to an alt(or alternative character) she was making specifically so that character could obtain that item's appearance.

A white, brief like, clothing item that looked remarkably similar to a caveman-esque Cloth Diaper…

…

Anteros was sitting in his room, computers currently turned off, clad in cloth-like backed diaper and black shirt emblazoned with the Teenage Mutant Ninja Turtles, in front of a whiteboard adorned with several plan ideas for how to stop the coming storm crossed out upon it. "It's a pickle Boss, that's for sure," Maux said casually, himself with a onesie covering his diaper with the logo for their MMO characters' faction, The Swarm, embossed upon its front.

He'd already crossed out plans involving putting it out over the internet, appealing to potentially sympathetic parties like Hades, even engaging in domestic terrorism to stop the flow of fossil fuels. Everything either involved sparking a war, potentially getting caught, or was simply too big an operation for a single Cupid and a Goblin.

"Ugh, I give up man," Ant said as he raised a sippy cup filled with Kool-aid into the air, "A toast. To the end of the world!" Anteros called out as he took a swallow of the sugary liquid, Maux reaching for a baby bottle similarly filled and took a drink himself. "Don't suppose anyone's gonna port Humans to another world when this one's destroyed, eh?" Maux said, referring to The Swarm's backstory.

"Not likely," Ant replied solemnly, taking another sip. "It's not like they didn't have a good run," Ant opined. The humans probably could've avoided it themselves if they weren't so enslaved to their fuel sources. It's too bad they didn't have access to magic like Ant's own kind. Though considering they were being manipulated into their demise by Ant's own kind the thought was somewhat ironic.

"HEY LISTEN!" Ant's phone called out, the videogame fairy's voice indicating he'd received a text message. It was from Nereid,

Hey, meet me at the Metalworking building on campus. Come equipped. I've got a plan. <3

"Well, what was it?" Maux cried impatiently, a bit cranky with the end of the world eminent and all. "It's Nereid!" Ant replied, his heart fluttering at her use of a heart emote at the end of her message, but no less ecstatic that she'd come up with something. "She's got a plan bud! She says to meet her at the Metalworking building, armed," Anteros continued. "Alright! First good news all day Boss!" Maux said, jumping up and doing a very goblin-esque dance on Ant's bed, all the more cute clad in his onesie.

Before too long diaper changes were had, logistics plans were made, along with a dufflebag prepared and filled with supplies and extra diapers. Anteros wearing a navy blue shirt and navy blue pants over his mission diaper, crossbow pistol bolts strapped to his thigh, and crossbow pistol strapped to the other, and Maux opted out of his usual onesie, and instead let his diaper show, wearing a powder blue baby's hoodie shirt emblazoned HUGS in red lettering, a golden earring in one of his long green ears, traditional Goblin footwear protecting the tops of his feet and armbands containing spell components for more complicated craftwork.

It was overcast when the two of them arrived at the Metalworking building on campus, the duffle swung over one of Ant's shoulders, and Maux riding atop the other, Diaper and for the first time in a long time, hope, projecting from him. It fit the mood.

The building they arrived to was a nondescript cube of a structure, with a stucco-like exterior, inside was a garage like interior where various blacksmithing and engineering supplies were housed. Normally it would be busy with students making various school projects in preparation for careers in the trade, however this time of year even College was on summer break so the campus was completely deserted.

Deserted save for three figures smiling and waving at Anteros and Maux as they approached the building. One was definitely a sight for Ant's sore eyes, Nereid, decked out in full gold plate armor, warhammer in one hand, buckler shield in the other. It didn't do anything to show off her figure, however it was clearly magicked to be much lighter than traditional human plate, and Nereid stood with hip at full sway. The other two figures caught Ant by surprise until he realized who they were. The other two members of their RP gaming party.

The short dwarf girl could've passed for decent Gimli cosplay with her full beard and helmet, the only thing breaking the illusion being her soft rosy cheeks, pink eyeshadow, and bright pink lipstick. Her axe held at the ready looked to be able to take down anyone as well as the famous Tolkien dwarves ever could.

"Yo buddy!" the third figured called out as Ant and Maux approached, unlike the other two, he wore nothing but a simple pair of black jeans. Now that Ant could see him standing, he was incredibly tall, even to relatively tall Anteros, and his well chiselled body was completely covered in thick rocky plates all over his skin and face.

Anteros at first was a bit dismayed that others were going to be in on this plan, he didn't want to endanger anyone, nor did he want a repeat of Erichthonius(the thought made him wince, he was presumably their friend after all), but the dismay was quickly dispelled when he realized that if Nereid trusted them and thought they were needed, he had no business questioning it himself.

He was going to correct one mistake though, "I'm sorry ab-" Ant began but he was interrupted by the rocky giant holding up a hand, "Don't worry about it man, after Nereid told us what he did...," and the giant winced himself at that point. "No, no, no, I mean, yeah, I'm sorry about that, but what I'm actually saying is, I'm such a clueless dick that I never asked either of your names," Anteros said, somewhat relieved that the bit of awkwardness was at least gonna be different.

The giant chuckled, "I'm Emet, and this is my girlfriend, Sindri," Emet said as Sindri gave a squeaky "hi!" Ant thought she sounded a bit like Bubbles from the Powerpuff girls.

"Alright Kiddo, we can small talk later," Nereid said before Anteros could respond, hefting her warhammer and giving him a smirk. "Right," Sindri piped in, "any minute now a connection to the Bifrost should be appearing, be warned though, there's a reason I told you to come armed," she said as a rainbow appeared in the sky and as Ant's eyes followed it, it seemed to envelope them all in an otherworldly glow in all colors of the spectrum. Ant was sure he was seeing colors that even Olympiad eyes were not meant to see in extreme ranges as the five of them were pulled up and out of their own reality, the swirling colors looking not unlike being pushed into hyperspace, and transported them onto another...

Chapter 15

"Ben-zonna! You could've warned me it was gonna be this damned cold!?" Emet yelled out on arrival. "Uh, I tried, remember? If I recall correctly, you told me 'Ha, my body IS plate, Sindri!'" the dwarf girl retorted, mocking Emet's voice sarcastically. "Yeah, I thought you meant for armor, I didn't know it was gonna be cold!" Emet continued to argue, and the two went back and forth for a bit as Anteros took in their surroundings.

Ant was pretty cold himself despite being fully clothed. The area they landed in was a heavily wooded forest, and snow covered the ground in a thick powdery sheet. If he wasn't on a mission Ant might have been tempted to sit and admire it. The forest was almost too picturesque and wouldn't have been out of place on Human Christmas cards. "I feel his pain, Boss," Maux whispered in Ant's ear, shivering as he'd chosen to go with just shirt and diaper himself.

"Quiet you two!" Nereid yelled out, commanding attention. "Sindri, what is it we're supposed to be on the lookout for?" she asked as all of a sudden the shivering stopped on Ant's shoulder. "Buddy, you...?" Ant had only just turned to see the normally goblin green Maux had turned a solid icy blue, "There, frozen veins takes care of it," SMASH!, a glass goblet shattered onto a nearby tree just as the mage got his sentence out.

"THAT!" Sindri shouted as she raised her axe into the air, "Yoth da Narvak!" she cried out as she charged, axe first into the treeline. Ant turned to see Emet shrug and run in after her, "Honey boo boo! Wait!" the rocky giant ran after her at a sprint. "Well, once more into the breach, eh?" Nereid said with a smirk as she lowered a classical Corinthian helm over her head and raised her own Warhammer high and ran through the treeline.

"Well, Boss?" Maux said plainly, as Anteros nodded and pushed through two of the trees himself, snow falling onto the ground beneath his own ice crunching steps, Crossbow pistol at the ready. What he saw on arrival threw him for a loop, his companions were scraping their way through hundreds of...gnomes? There were four long tables stretched out before a large wooden building, with a massive barrel at the end of each table. Anteros tried to slip into the wake of Nereid, herself smacking away gnomes left and right as if she was hitting golf balls with her warhammer. Ant tried to pick one to aim at, but there were too many. "Oomph! Boss!" Maux called out as a gnome had jumped onto the goblin's back, it snarled loud with drool oozing from its face, exposing tons of tiny sharp teeth as it tried to bite at Maux's ear. An icy blast caused Ant's neck to recoil instinctively as Maux cast another spell, this one freezing the gnome solid and propelling him out and away from the two of them.

It would almost have been comical seeing his friends smacking away what looked like ordinary garden gnomes for all intents and purposes, save for the freakishly snarling, biting, bloodthirsty faces attached to all of them. Maux shot an icy orb out in front of Ant, freezing any gnomes who got too near just as it had the one that jumped on Ant's back, as Anteros began to take aim in earnest, popping off arrows that exploded with tiny fireballs on impact, offering a steep contrast to Maux's icy magic as they made their way up to the middle of the table line, Nereid sprinting in front of them as fast as she could go.

Anteros was starting to be afraid the party might start to be overwhelmed as more and more gnomes made it past Maux's ice ball and onto his legs, biting at his ankles like tiny bear-traps when the corner of his eye caught Emet near one of the Barrels at the end of the table. The rocky giant reared back with his fist and pounded it straight into the barrel, busting a massive hole in it as pressurized Beer shot out like a firehose into the gnomish crowds. The creatures' eyes widened as the smell of alcohol tinged the air. "HRAGH!" they cried out as the tiny statuesque figures hurreled themselves into the onrushing beer stream.

"What. The Hades. Was that!?" Anteros exclaimed between pants as he ascended the steps to the wooden house, some warmth spreading between his legs as clearly he'd wet his diaper on the charge.

"Gnomes," Sindri said plainly. "Yeah, I think we could figure that out for ourselves," Nereid said sarcastically. "Annoying buggers," Sindri continued, "They're normally pretty good natured, like little beer-swilling cats, but in the presence of ma-gic!," she said, mockingly dragging out the word with some annoyance directed at Maux, who was still riding atop Ant's shoulder, though also seeming a bit wet himself. "They go nuts. We keep them around as a bit of an alarm system in case something slips past Heimdall's gaze," Sindri continued.

"But I thought nothing could slip past him?" Emet asked. "Well, yeah, but Asgardians also like to have a bit of fun on the way in too, and smacking gnomes is somewhat of a pastime," Sindri said with a laugh.

"Anyway, welcome to the Bifrost office," Sindri said brightly, "If you look up you can see Yggdrasil spread out across the sky," she continued, pointing up. Anteros looked skyward for the first time since their arrival. He thought it was just night, but now he could see in this realm it would be perpetually "night", as streaking like tendrils across what passed for a horizon on this world were tons of branch like arms, filled with otherworldly stars and constellations, at the center of which, looking not unlike an Earth full-moon was presumably Valhalla at the center of the tree where Odin resides.

The door of the wooden dwelling swung open to reveal a black haired dwarf standing in the doorway, beard even longer than Sindri's that extended ankle length. "Sindri!" the voice was deeper, but most certainly feminine as she embraced the dwarf before her. "Hi mom," Sindri replied as sweetly as she could given the circumstances.

"You must be Emet and Nereid and…" the Dwarf said as she looked at each of the members of the group. "This is Anteros and Maux," Sindri said, "more friends of mine."

"Come in, come in," the older dwarf insisted, ushering them into the door where a roaring fire was going at the end of the room, producing much needed warmth. It smelled delicious, as a cauldron was bubbling over that fire, and the room was filled with comfortable looking armchairs, though in odd proportions for Ant's frame. "I'm sorry I haven't been able to meet you, but the Bifrost constantly needs maintenance," she said as she hurried to stir the cauldron. It was at this point that Anteros noticed the far wall of the cabin, it had what appeared for all intents and purposes an old fashioned telephone switchboard, an array of cables and wires sticking out of it and into the wall.

Anteros diaper felt like it was starting to sag and though he'd brought extra diapers, he wasn't sure where to get changed at. Nereid clearly must have seen his eyes darting around because she spoke up to the older dwarf, "Uh, Ms....?"

"Call me Edda," she said sweetly as she brushed off some dust that had begun to accumulate on her beard. "Edda, is there a place Ant can, um, get his diaper changed?" Nereid replied.

"What?" she looked taken aback. "Yeah, I'm a Cupid," Anteros said and he could tell Edda looked to stifle a laugh, but was polite enough to hold it back, "Well, I haven't had need of diapers 'round here since Sindri was a wee babe," she spoke up, "And the only facilities I've got is a latrine in the back," she continued. "Yer prettymuch lookin at my dwellings here," she finished, gesturing at the single large room they were standing in.

It was Maux who ultimately took the initiative, pulling one of Ant's diapers out of his bag. "If yous guys could uh, turn around maybe?" Maux's gravelly voice sounded out as he twirled his finger in a circular motion. Edda audibly gasped at this point, just now noticing the Goblin's presence, his own diaper exposed but quickly regained her composure. Once their compatriots had turned for some privacy, Maux undid Ant's pants and directed him by the hand to lie down, untaping his diaper once he did. Ant blushed a bit as he could tell a couple of them peaked out of sheer curiosity. Nereid winked when she did, before blushing herself.

Once Maux had finished wiping him, he applied rash cream and powder and taped the new diaper on Anteros as he got up and Maux helped pull up his pants and reattach the weapons mounts back upon his person. Anteros then pulled a baby diaper from the duffle and returned the favor to his companion, a much easier task since Maux had chosen to go pantless for this trip.

"All done?" Edda called out, as their friends turned to once again face him, Anteros turning a beet red out of embarrassment. "Alright, alright, down to business" Sindri said with a wave, clearly wanting to spare Anteros in addition to actually being in a hurry.

"Yes," Edda said brightly, clearly an attentive employee, "T'will take a moment to transfer to Mount Olympus but we can get you there. We get you anywhere!" she said sweetly as she pulled a few switches on the switchboard and moved a few wires.

As before a rainbow descended on the party from above, though it seemed at least ten times brighter and more vivid this close to the source. Anteros looked over at Edda just long enough to see Sindri rip herself from Edda's grasp and leap into the Bifrost, "Sorry mom!" she called out as Edda's outstretched hand grasped nothing but air…

Chapter 16

If Asgard was a world of perpetual night, Olympus was its polar opposite, with bright golden rays shining down from the heavens. In front of them, in all its glory stood the Acropolis, or at least, what looked exactly like it. Structurally anyway, whereas most humans seemed to picture the ancient world in a pristine white, in reality it was bright and gaudily painted. Humans remembered history from the present, i.e. after the ancient devotees of the Olympiad religion had already fallen into disrepair. In Olympus, it was anything but.

The large columns were solid gold, with the mosaics and embossed sculptures in vibrant colors depicting the glory of Rome or Athens at its height. The near ubiquitous cloud cover giving it a bit of a stained glass cathedral look than the Christmas card they'd just departed.

"Well, I guess the phrase 'tone it down' never made it to this neck of the multiverse, eh?" Emet said at the sight, the rock-man shielding his eyes from the blinding sun. "So where do we go now?" Sindri asked. "I'm not entirely sure," Nereid responded, "I've never actually been to Olympus before." Neither had Anteros. They didn't normally let half-breeds like them enter into the kingdom of the Gods, and the rare occasions when a Hercules or a Perseus did make it into the heavens it was a truly big deal.

They were standing on a cobblestone road that was encrusted with jewels and rubies between what looked like the Parthenon on one side, and the Pantheon on the other. "Well, somehow we need to let Jupiter know of Juno and Neptune's plans," Anteros said, though it occurred to him that it was a lot less helpful once he'd said it out loud. "Boss, I think we know that much," Maux said derisively, but Ant was really at a loss here. He didn't exactly expect to get this far, he was no Hercules, he was just a cupid. *I'm still in diapers,* he thought somewhat sarcastically, crinkle serving as emphasis.

SMAINGK! The clanging vibrations of metal slamming on metal ran through their bodies like it was about to register on the richter scale. Ant turned along with the others and his mouth dropped open. Two massive cyclops had just closed the pearly gates on them, and from the two structures on either side emerged more of the monocular creatures. "CHEESE IT!" Maux yelled out, "Split up!" Nereid shouted in kind as they ran in opposite directions for various alleyways, hoping to escape their would-be captors. Ant had just enough reflex to pop a shot off at one of the Cyclops by the gate, hitting him square in his eyeball with a BANG! blinding him instantly.

Ant stopped to pant between two smaller buildings(though still very much in the style of the Pantheon) in a bit of shade and realized his goblin companion was no longer riding on his shoulder, in fact he wasn't anywhere! He almost called out for him, but realized that might be even worse, if Maux had escaped, Anteros didn't want to call any attention to him.

Ant ultimately decided he would have to move on with the mission, no matter how badly the worry for his friends filled his stomach with burning acid. Jupiter might be able to secure their release in gratitude even if they were captured. Of course he'd have to figure out where the king of the Gods was even currently located. The alleyway he'd fled to was towards the right of where they were standing, though he had no way to tell true cardinal directions, he reasoned he would label it "east" from where they were standing, the gate "south", and he wanted to go "north" from it, figuring the throne would be located at the center of the polis.

At a brisk pace he rounded a corner and departed in search of that direction. As the rays of sunshine began to penetrate the shadows of the buildings of the Acropolis indicating he was nearing some open ground several figures approached him from the shadows causing Ant to stop dead in his tracks.

"There he is!" one of them called out, pointing in his direction to command his comrades. They were dressed in full Hoplite armor, with tridents and shields as weaponry. Loading up an arrow, Anteros whispered a spell causing it to glow a purple hue and fired in their general direction. When the arrow hit the ground it ignited a foul smelling smoke as Ant ran for it in the other direction, only to come face to face with another contingent of the exact same guards. He was caught in their mousetrap.

Ant looked up, the domed roof of the Pantheon esque building looked like his only escape route. Godly strength aiding him he lept up, grabbing hold of the edge of the roof and hauled himself up to its surface, another foul smell greeting him on arrival.

Ant sighed, *of all times to mess a diaper*, and took off as briskly as he could in the general direction of "north" while trying to ignore the chafing…

…

"Honey, I don't know if this is such a good idea!" Emet called out as Sindri planted an axe into the chest of the nearest Hoplite in her vicinity. "Prir!" was all she said in return, as another Hoplite swung in their direction, prompting a swift punch through his helmet and into his skull from Emet. "Fjhornir!" she called out, giving him a thumbs up.

"Anymore takers wanna give us a try!?" she shrieked in her high pitched tone. "Don't you think we oughta go find the others?" Emet continued to plead. "A proper Dwarf does not run!" she retorted, "I won't let them take us!" and almost on cue another wave of hoplites rounded the corner to their current position. They had taken the left side towards the Parthenon from Anteros and rather than escaping the trap, Sindri preferred a more direct approach, much to Emet's chagrin.

"Yoth da Narvak!" Sindri cried as she parried a stab attempt from a trident and rolled to implant the Axe into the Hoplite's back, "Fimm!"

Emet's shoulders slumped with a sigh before he reared back and punched another Hoplite, and kicked another across from him. Before he could land another blow, however, he felt a large weight fall on his back and he kneeled to the ground, followed by another and another. The Hoplites decided to try and gang-tackle him, but Emet pulled all of his reserves to thrust upward with explosive force, causing the various Hoplites to go careening in other directions.

"We need higher ground!" Sindri called out, "up the steps!" With that she proceeded to run into the Parthenon itself, Emet following suit. "Wow, bubbla, that's gotta make at least Nihu!" she said sweetly, admiring his handiwork. "Yeah, let's not let it go to our heads though," he replied, turning to run deeper into the building.

Though somewhat shaded compared to the vibrancy of the rest of Olympus itself, it was still impressively lit, the golden interior reflecting the sunlight to create an almost sepia-toned glow that seemed to accentuate the various tapestries, statues, and mosaics depicting various victories throughout the Olympiads history. It was an impressive shrine if Emet did say so himself.

He didn't have time to reflect on the artistry of the building, however, as boots could be heard echoing from all corners of the Parthenon. Sindri let out another battlecry as she ran once more into the fray, and Emet squared up, ready to take on the next comer himself.

But something…odd, caught the corner of his vision. One of the golden statues it, moved? A Trident blow reached out to grab his face but before Emet could even react, the Hoplite warrior froze and turned to stone right before his eyes and Emet found himself staring into the screaming face of a severed head, covered in hissing snakes which bore holes into his soul and he instantly recognized what he was looking at. It was a statue of Perseus! "Sindri, close your eyes!" The Medusa head must not have affected Emet considering he was already made of stone, but his beloved wouldn't be so lucky, and neither had the Hoplite that tried to attack him.

Emet let out a howl as Sindri yelled "What?" and he punched straight into the metallic face of Perseus. The golden statue merely tanked his blow as no mortal could and a squeal sounded behind him as Emet turned to see Sindri, eyes glued shut, several Hoplites finally having overpowered her with this newfound sight advantage.

Emet screamed as he ran at them to rescue her but collapsed in pain as a golden sword ran him through the back. Looking up from the ground his last glimpse was the sight of a colossal Cyclops striding into the Parthenon, his large steps echoing across the golden walls as he laughed heartily.

"Looks like we finally got'cha, heh heh heh…"

…

Anteros found it a bit difficult to crest the massive dome of the Panthcon as it was incredibly smooth, but fortunately its size made it feel a lot less steep than it might otherwise have been, combined with his own otherworldly agility and balance it was nonetheless traversable.

Just when he began to feel some level of confidence to his present situation, heavy diaper and all, he almost fell head first off the edge of the building when he'd reached the other side. Below a group of Hoplites were squaring off with a much heavier armored golden warrior...wielding a Warhammer!

Nereid swung at a Hoplite, knocking him back, and another, and another, but every time two to three more took the last's place as they slowly began to gain ground upon her. Ant loaded up an arrow and whispered another spell at it and took aim just behind their line, a BANG! sounded as a bright flash drew the attention of the Hoplites to their rear and Anteros, loading another bolt as he did so, took a leap off the side of the building, landing atop the head of one of the Hoplites. Something in his subconscious taking some pride in the fact that his diaper's waistband held in his present mess, considering the force sent a little of it up his buttocks, but was prevented from proceeding up his backside.

Taking aim with his crossbow pistol Ant nailed a Hoplite through the eyehole on his helmet, smirked at Nereid, who grabbed him by the arm and dragged him down the alleyway and away from the pursuing Hoplites. "You idiot! I had them taken care of, you could've gotten yourself killed! You're supposed to focus on the mission!" she snarled at him angrily. When Nereid finally stopped towards another building, she smacked him hard on the hand, "Don't you do that again!" she exclaimed, and Ant hung his head a minute before sheepishly replying, "Sorry…" but at that point she hugged him tight, though it was a little awkward against the heavy plate armor covering her body.

"Did you poop?" Nereid said, sniffing the air a bit. "Yeah, it happens," and Ant averted his gaze a bit, unable to stop the involuntary embarrassment. "It's alright, maybe we can find a spot to hide and change you in here," Nereid said as she directed him into the building in front of them. Though a columned structure straight out of classical antiquity like the rest of the ubiquitous structures throughout Olympus, this one was notably different than the others, as it seemed to be made of a solid white limestone. Save for the bright red painting of its roof, and multicolored figures adorning its front archway, it would almost look like the ruins so fetishized by the Humans of Earth.

As they climbed the steps Anteros suddenly started feeling around his chest. He'd lost the duffle! "Shit!" Ant cursed. "What?" Nereid inquired inquisitively. "We can't change me, at some point I must've lost the duffle, and," Anteros felt around his thigh at that point, "I've only got a few bolts left on me, the rest of my ammo was in there too," Ant continued, a bit dejected.

"Well you can just summon your diaper bag, right?" Nereid asked, Anteros figured she must have seen it in action at the self storage. "No, the coin's bonded to Maux, not me. Only he can recite the incantation," Ant said, a pang of regret hitting him square in the chest. He didn't yet know what happened to his Goblin friend.

"Oh Ant! I'm so-" Nereid started but Anteros cut her off with a wave of his hand, it hurt a little much to talk about, and they had bigger problems at present. The building they'd entered was weirdly pitch dark with shadow, having a solid roof and none of the golden adornment seen across the rest of the landscape. At the center was a large statue on a raised platform of a humanoid figure driving a chariot pulling behind a massive circular mirror.

It hit Anteros like a ton of bricks what temple they were in at the sight, "Nereid, we should get out of here!" he cried out, but it was too late. With a startling suddenness the mirror began to pivot and the chariot began to move, directing a powerful beam of light from its surface, burning a pattern into the limestone below. Anteros instinctively hopped to the side with a bit of a squish from his soggy diaper, as a burn mark etched itself right between where his legs were previously occupying, Nereid barrel rolling off in the other direction.
Hoplites descended upon their location from all sides of the building adding to their increasingly harrowed movements as Ant attempted to dodge trident strikes(no small feat when one is unable to close their legs) and Nereid began swatting them away with her Warhammer. Every single movement punctuated by the stony gaze of the statue of Apollo directing his sunlight like a deadly lazer at every attempt to anticipate a Hoplite movement.

Thud! Thud! Thud! the sound of thunderous footsteps abounded off the walls, causing Anteros to get singed by the light, destroying the integrity of his diaper as a mixture of urine, feces, and absorbent gel fell to the floor. Before Anteros could even react to this mortifying turn of events a pair of hands grasped him and brought him up face to face with a mono-orbital eye currently adorned with a sickeningly cocky grin.

"ANTEROS!" Nereid yelled from behind, leaping towards him, lazer leaving a melted gash across her breastplate as she did so, but it was too late. The Hoplites were already subduing her as the life was being squeezed out of Ant's body.

"You're MINE boy!" the Cyclops yelled, deafening Anteros this close to his face as his bearhug slowly made Ant's desperate gasps for breath shorter and shorter.

"This one's fer my brother." the Cyclops whispered into Ant's ear as the light dimmed to nothing and Anteros lost all conscious perception of this world…

Chapter 17

He was….floating? Buoyantly in the air in a lazy up and down motion. *Am I dead?* Anteros thought. No, that didn't make sense. Where's the ferryman? Ant shook his head and blinked a few times, eyesight finally returning to him. He was apparently in some sort of large jail cell, gently…flying? He was hovering a few feet off the ground. He could feel the rhythmic swishing of his wings. *I've got wings!?* He looked to either side of him and indeed flapping near his head were a pair of perfectly angelic wings holding him aloft.

What he did not have was any clothes on, save for a swaddling of cloth around his crotch area. He was, with the exception of his height and lithe frame, the perfect image of a Cherub for the first time in his life. He was almost involuntarily ecstatic before he saw what was going on in the corner of the cell. Nereid was standing hunched over a pair of figures, the armor on her upper body removed, a simple t-shirt on, torn slightly exposing a bit of her bra. He didn't have time to dwell on it as the full force of what he was seeing slowly came into focus. Sindri was there in the corner, tending to an egregious looking wound on the rock giant Emet.

"W…" "Wrhat Hrappened?" Anteros' gargled voice finally escaped his lips.

"We don't know, they brought you in that way," Nereid said as she turned to face him, a very purple bruise enveloping her left eye.

Without a lot of thought Anteros instinctively flew over to the three, floating mere inches above the ground at this point, he could hear Sindri sobbing and he nearly broke down himself. "Guys, I'm sorry, it's all my fault, I don't know what to…" but

Anteros' apology was cut off by what sounded like a small child's chuckle at the bars of their cell.

"I'm what happened," the voice that spoke was much deeper than the laugh. It was gravelly even, kind of like Maux's were it not for how much lower pitched it was. Anteros turned to face it and found himself staring at a perfectly chubby baby, with wings and swaddling, floating not unlike Ant himself on the other side of the bars. It would almost have been funny were it not for the circumstances. The "baby" was bright red haired, olive skinned, with piercing blue eyes. He looked not unlike Baby Herman of *Who Framed Roger Rabbit?* fame.

"I have the power to do that now, Ant," the "baby" said with a smile, pointing at Ant's wings. Anteros was a bit shocked to hear his name as the pieces slowly began to fall into place. "That's right. I am your father," he said. Anteros couldn't help it, he flew right at the bars, grabbing them and shaking. "Listen! There's a plot to take down Jupiter! We're here to warn him! Please, you've gotta help us!" Ant spit it out at lightning speed, all pretense thrown out the window as desperate pleading entered his thoughts above all others.

"Hah! Bwahahaha!" his father was laughing a bit too hard and a wet spot formed at the center of his swaddling diaper. "You-You thought? Hahaha!" the laughter took away all of Ant's feelings, replacing them with an empty pit throughout his body.

His father produced a Cigar and a match from thin air and lit it as he began to take puffs, "You thought you were gonna stop us? A bunch of kids and half-breeds stop Juno and Neptune? Ha! Boy have you got this all wrong," his father said, finally stopping the chuckles.

Anteros couldn't believe it, they'd already lost before they started. Why couldn't he see it sooner? Of course they wouldn't just stumble into the hostile takeover of the cosmos! Waves of guilt and depression washed over Anteros as a numbness started to spread outward from his chest to his limbs. It was all a waste.

"Chin up boyo," his father spoke up, picking up on the vibes being given off by Ant's emotional state. "I'm here to help actually," he said fluttering a bit, brightening up with an extremely babyish smile spread across his face exposing a mouthful of child's teeth. "You like dem wings?" his father began, "your daddy here can make 'em permanent."

"Your friends? I can heal 'em. Think about it! No more bullying! Juno promised me a place atop the pantheon! Gods'll have take us seriously!" his father's voice heightened as he delved into his sales pitch.

Images began to flood Anteros' mind, the Daimone from the warehouse, the Cyclops, Erichthonius, the faces of a hundred bullies from his childhood, teasing him about his diapers, about his parentage. He could picture them all surrounding him, laughing at his leaky diaper. An anger swelled up within him like a roaring fire. He understood why his father did it. He could feel it, the burning desire for vengeance, to turn the tables on the world for a change!

"Do you think I wanted to abandon you? Jupiter wrote those rules! We can fix it! We can rewrite history in our image! All you gotta do is join us…son," and the little cherub lit up with an extremely leery wide-eyed smile, one could almost see the green emanating off of it as he extended a baby sized arm for a handshake.

Anteros almost grabbed it without hesitation. The desire to do it burned in all his neurons, every nerve ending longed to touch it, unnaturally so. But the sight of Nereid shaking her head in horror shocked him, Sindri even was looking his way now, pink makeup streaming down her face and into her beard, Emet's heavy labored breathing finally starting to stabilize.

A different set of images resounded in Ant's mind. His mother at his apartment tending to Maux's mom, Nereid without hesitation changing his diapers, Sindri and Emet laughing around the RP table, his friends had accepted him without question. The image of the world flooding and humans drowning as death and destruction reigned swirled into focus. A different feeling entirely spread through his body now.

"People," Anteros looked back at his father, still beaming in his direction, "People are gonna get hurt, aren't they?" he asked with grim determination.

"What? The Earth?" his father's expression shifted to one of disgust, "A bunch of humans? Who cares? It'll be reborn! You could be a God at my side!"

"I'm sorry but, I'm gonna have to turn you down," Anteros replied solemnly.

"Pity," the cherub said, his expression returning to blank as he snapped his fingers and Anteros fell with a thud onto the floor, smacking his chin hard on the pavement. "You were nothin but a failed experiment. Now rot there, until you die!"

and the cherub dropped his cigar onto ground where it smoldered as he left into the darkened hallway, the unnatural green following him out of the building they were housed in.

The wings had become a brittle plastic that crumbled as Nereid rushed to Ant's side, holding him in close as the Cupid found himself in a broken fetal position in her arms.

"Hehehehe…"

Anteros picked up at the sound, *where was it coming from?* He couldn't see anything beyond the bars of the cell, but the laughter was still emanating. "You look like the front of a box of candy hearts!" said a high pitched gravelly New Jersey accent, followed swiftly by a hoodie being lowered and a Goblin head with brightly glowing red eyes floating about two feet off the ground.

When the eyes dimmed the rest of the diaper clad Goblin came into focus. "Man, fuck you!" Anteros said involuntarily with a smile returning to his face, crawling as fast as he could to the bars and embracing his friend in the hardest hug he thought he'd ever given.

"I thought I lost you," Anteros said, tears welling up in his eyes. "You and all of Mount Olympus," Maux said, "there's so much magic floating around here, nobody noticed a trace o'little ol' me, heh!" and with that the Goblin sat cross legged on the floor in front of the cell.

"Ya a khetsaram kiranann du…Ya a khetsaram kiranann du….Ya a khetsaram kiranann du…."

As Maux chanted a grey-green diaper bag popped into existence within his lap. "Always keep a well stocked diaper bag," Maux chuckled, and Anteros, though he'd mentioned it earlier, was still somewhat amazed the coin worked even upon Mount Olympus.

Swinging the bag across his back(no small feat considering it was almost as tall as he was) Maux blinked out of existence and reappeared on their side of the bars. "And for my next trick!" Maux said brightly as he whispered some ancient Olympian and a biscuit like muffin appeared in his hand and he waddled it over to the stone giant in the corner of the room. It was actually kind of cute with his exposed diaper drooping slightly as the goblin did so.

"Eat this," Maux said as he pushed it into Emet's mouth, "it'll restore your health," Maux continued as Sindri rubbed the giant's throat to encourage him to swallow. Almost instantaneously Emet's eyes fluttered open and he coughed a few times. "The rest of you grab a crumb or two, it'll help," and Sindri ate a bite, followed by Nereid whose eye went from a deep purple to a bit of a pale green. "What'd I miss?" Emet said groggily as his coughing subsided, followed swiftly by Sindri embracing him hard and kissing him deeply before anyone could answer.

"Let's give them a moment," Nereid said as she took hold of the diaper bag and pulled out an adult diaper from the center pocket, and after some wriggling to remove Ant's wet swaddling began using the wipes to clean his diaper area, then taped a fresh diaper upon him. Anteros did feel much better afterwards, he had to admit. Nereid then removed a baby diaper from the bag and repeated the favor for Maux, who'd apparently pooped in his at some point.

Maux smiled and muttered a "thanks" before blinking back out of existence and reappearing on the other side of the bars.

"So, how you gonna get us outta here buddy?" Anteros asked with a renewed vigor.

"I'm gonna do you one better," Maux replied, but then he frowned just a little, "I gotta do it alone though, sorry."

"What?" Anteros was genuinely confused at this statement.

"I think I got a plan to square this circle," the Goblin said with a smirk before his eyes began to glow, and raising his hoodie he shimmered out of sight once more...

Chapter 18

Four Hours Earlier

"CHEESE IT!" Maux called out, followed in short order by Nereid yelling for them to split up. The Cyclops' club smashed down beside Anteros as he made a beeline to the right near the Pantheon looking building. The resounding impact knocked the small Goblin loose from his companion's shoulder, but he caught himself with his cat-like reflexes on the fall.

Maux's first instinct was to go chasing after his Boss, but unlike the Godly imbued abilities of Anteros, which lent the Cupid incredible feats of agility, what Maux gained in catlike reflexes, he lacked in catlike speed. The tabletop RP world got Goblin walking speed right on the money. Instead he made a snap decision to raise his hoodie, and muttering an ancient Olympian incantation as he waddled away from the fray shimmered out of sight. For all intents and purposes disappeared from this plane of reality.

As he strolled along the jewel encrusted pathway down the center of the polis, he took in his gaudy surroundings, lit brilliantly by the otherworldly sunshine. The hoodie's power didn't render him truly invisible, per se, if one focused directly on his personage one might see a bit of a flicker for a moment. Maux likened it to getting a floater in one's eye. But at just over two feet tall in a land of Gods and Giants it was unlikely anyone was going to be focusing on him anytime soon.

All around him he could see Hoplites, *the Putties of the Olympiad world,* Maux thought derisively. Maux was confident his compatriots could take them, it was the Cyclopes they'd have to steer clear from.

Maux decided to help them out in that regard as he skipped along the boulevard. Each Cyclops was at the end of alleyways barking orders at Hoplites like "Find them!" and "Keep your eyes open!" Maux thought it was odd the footsoldiers were all seemingly armed with Tridents, after all, wasn't the traditional Hoplite weapon a spear? For that matter, what were a bunch of Cyclopes doing ordering around Jupiter's foot soldiers? Something didn't add up, but Maux didn't dwell on it as there was a lot more fun to have.

With a sharp toothy grin, Maux fired a ring of frost at the nearest Cyclops, the Goblin remaining hidden beneath the Hoodie's magic. The Cyclops foot was frozen in place and he struggled to break it through, nearly tripping over himself to Maux's delight.

To the next Cyclops, Maux shot icicles onto the skirt of his centurion's outfit, causing it to slip downward and expose his buttocks to the Hoplites who couldn't help but laugh at their commander's misfortune. It was all Maux could do to keep from guffawing himself.

He was honestly having the time of his life, being the trickster was a Goblin's true passion after all. He enchanted an area in front of a group of Hoplites so that when they stepped upon it, they'd be overcome with the feeling that there were mines beneath their feet, and so when they did their bodies flung themselves outwards, though no real damage was done. Maux chuckled some more.

Just after he'd frozen another Cyclops helmet shut Maux stumbled upon a street sign written in Ancient Olympian. Included was a directory of the various buildings along the street, including the Parthenon, the Pantheon, several temples to minor Gods and heroes, and at the end of the street emblazoned in white-gold lettering advertised the Temple of Apollo. It was just above that building that interested Maux, however. Located directly next to the Temple was the Library of the Oracle.

"Take them alive, Neptune's orders!" a Cyclops shouted nearby. *Neptune's orders?* and all of a sudden the happiness drained from Maux's body. They were too late, the coup had already taken place. It was the only explanation for Neptune giving orders to the Hoplites. Shooting an ice slick down at the Cyclops feet caused him to bust his ass, but no chuckle escaped Maux's lips as he made a break for the library.

With a road made for strides that could reach upward of ten feet it was a wonder that Maux made it to the library at all, especially with the waddle of an increasingly heavy diaper making his own strides more and more difficult. He tried to speed up the process with intermittent teleports but he could only go so far with them. Still, after what felt like an eternity he arrived at a tall, golden columned building.

It would have been nearly indistinguishable from others were it not for a large sculpture of a scroll etched into the front facing of the building, as opposed to the usual painted mosaics adorning most of the other buildings down the jewel boulevard.

Inside was nearly deserted, save for a tall woman sitting atop a desk writing furiously upon a scroll. Presumably the Muse in charge, Maux reasoned. The Goblin's first move was to make his way towards the cartography section. He was well out of sight of the Muse at the front, and with the place deserted he decided to risk it and pull out a scroll.

This was no easy task of course, each of them was literally his size or larger, he had to whisper a transmogrify spell with each one he pulled to make it actually usable for someone his size, and every time he could swear the Muse would look up from her work. With so few other beings, even a trace as small as his might register. Every time she simply went back to her work, however.

The first was a map of the Aegean, the next a map of Hades, another was a map of Tartarus of all places, he almost chuckled at the next one he pulled, a hand-drawn map that looked like it was written in crayon that was directions to a Bacchus party, and finally he pulled out the one he was looking for: A map of Mount Olympus itself. With this he would be able to find Jupiter's palace, though he wasn't sure exactly what he'd do at this point when he got there.

With it transmogrified small enough, he tucked it neatly in the pocket of his hoodie. He'd just about gotten to the front entrance of the library when he stopped and looked behind him at the Muse furiously writing away at the desk. Naturally she was writing onto a scroll, but what caught Maux's eye was what she was copying from, as it really had no place in this world whatsoever.

It was a Book. Now, a book in a library normally wouldn't be exactly cause for alarm, but in Mount Olympus? Land of clay tablets and papyrus scrolls? *The fuck is she doing with a book in this Library?* He thought. Every fiber of his being was screaming at him to quit while he was ahead and just simply leave. He'd accomplished the task without being seen, he'd won, he had every reason to just go now.

But he didn't. He couldn't. Whether it be his naturally curious Goblin roots, his frazzled, jet lagged, world hopping brain, or just plain old lack of common sense, he strode confidently over to the olive wood desk. It was huge, he'd have to climb it if he wanted to see what the Muse was looking at. He didn't have the time or the tools to climb it though.

He lifted his armband up to his face and pulled a few spell components out of it, deciding it was time for some Goblin engineering, yo!

Placing a few ingredients, including black powder and nitroglycerin into a pouch, Maux breathed a silent prayer to any of the gods on this plane whom might be sympathetic to this cause, whispered a noise muffling spell, and slammed the pouch onto the ground beneath him causing a small explosion to erupt beneath his feet.

Maux was propelled upward, a little too high actually, and landed atop the desk with a bit of a thud. His knees buckled beneath him, and Maux was pretty sure he'd pooped his diaper on impact.

He silently dodged out of the way when the massive hand of the Muse came crashing down upon the desk. *Maybe she thought it was a bug*, Maux thought, *do they have bugs in Olympus?* immediately followed.

The Muse was black haired and clad in a toga, she was using a feather pen and inkwell to copy notes down onto a scroll, and beside her was a massive book. A human book, clearly transmogrified to be more her size.

Taking great care to avoid her arms, Maux climbed atop the exposed page and tried to figure out what he was looking at. And it didn't take him long to figure it out.

Maux grew up reading, it was the cardinal sin that damned his family in the eyes of his own people, and one thing he'd read countless times growing up was a simple tale about daring heroes, crippling hubris, and the folly of man. A story oddly appropriate to Olympus, but actually being a human tale with varying degrees of truth to it with regard to Olympiad history. And that tale was the one he was currently standing atop of watching a Muse copy notes onto a scroll from.

The Iliad

There could be little doubt that was what the story was, and little doubt as to what exactly had transpired in Olympus as far as Maux was concerned. "OOMPH!" the sound escaped his lips without Maux having any ability to stop it as he was flung off the book and onto the hard table below. The Muse looked a bit puzzled at the suddenly different weight of her flipped page, but was herself startled at a sudden explosion rocking the building, followed by a massive shout of "HUZZAH!" emanating from outside the Library.

Maux didn't stick around to find out what happened next, gathering his wits about him, he took off as fast as he could, loaded diaper swinging between his legs as he waddled hard towards the edge of the desk and leaped off of it, whispering a feather spell that caused him to keep his sprint going at an angle, depositing him softly upon the floor, where he promptly took off out the front entrance.

What he saw upon his exit, however, made him stop in his tracks. A Cyclops was carrying the limp body of his best friend, and a group of Hoplites were carrying the charred remains of his best friend's would be girlfriend behind him.

FUCK!!

Maux no longer gave a damn about the mission. Keeping as silently as he could he followed the contingent of Olympiad thugs as they turned right down yet another jewel encrusted boulevard. Burdened as they were with bodies, and no longer being in any particular hurry, following was much easier, even at Goblin speed.

Maux moved silently as their party entered into a building that read "Prison" in ancient olympian. It was a solid grey building, though again, adorned with columns and mosaics as the others. Upon entry the Hoplites split off and marched down a hallway, but the Cyclops went in a different direction to the left. Maux sighed, he would feel bad about abandoning Nereid to whatever fate befell her, but even he couldn't be in two places at once and with a heavy heart chose to follow his buddy. At the very least he was relatively certain she would live, after all, if they wanted to kill her they could have already while she was unconscious. *Neptune's orders*, the Goblin thought wryly as the Cyclops rounded another corner to a row of offices.

This building seemed to be scaled a bit smaller than the Library had been, seemingly built to house mortal prisoners that lacked the reality distorting effect of Godly beings. But the office that the Cyclops stopped in front of was actually almost comically small compared to the other offices in the row. It was almost normal size for Maux.

When the door opened a flying baby came out of it. *A cherub?* Maux thought. He'd never actually seen one, after all, Anteros was abandoned as a child, and Maux's own realm had its own pantheon separate from Earth's. But he'd read their descriptions plenty of times as Earth books were relatively common from raiding on that world by denizens of his. After all, human myths abound for the exploits of his people upon theirs.

What happened next moved Maux from merely inquisitive to downright shocked. First the cherub pulled off Ant's pants, and it was at that point the sickly smell hit him. Whatever had attacked his friends hit them with something hot, as the putrid odor of burnt feces and melted plastic was nearly inescapable once he'd focused on it. The Cherub shook his head and snapped his fingers. The pulverized diaper and pants disappeared, including Ant's weapons as they were replaced by swaddling clothes.

The Cherub said something unintelligible to Maux's ears, even as a fluent speaker of Ancient Olympian, and wings sprouted from the back of Anteros. Maux's eyes went wide with shock, the now mostly naked Anteros was floating above the floor on flapping wings as the Cherub took him by the hand and lead him down the hallway to an awaiting Cyclops. It was an interesting sight, a flying baby leading a swaddled flying young adult down a hallway by the hand.

The Cherub watched as the Cyclops placed Anteros in a cell, where Maux was now aware his friends had been taken into custody.

The Cherub waited for a long time, studying Anteros, just out of sight of anyone in the cellblock. It was then that the pieces began to fall into place for Maux. This Cherub was Ant's father, and before long Anteros had awakened and the Cherub floated on to the entrance of the cell, guffawing when Ant attempted to plead with him.

I've got a bad feeling about this, Maux thought, though he didn't dare reveal himself in the presence of the Cherub. As much as he looked like a baby on the outside, he was still a God and could make short work of all of them here if he so desired.

Don't do it Ant, it's a trap! Maux thought as the Cherub offered his best friend the Faustian bargain. But much to Maux's surprise(he himself even felt an unnatural desire to accept the Cherub's deal against his own thoughts), Anteros turned him down! Maux's chest swelled with pride as the Cherub left dejected, though the Goblin winced when he saw Ant's chin smack the floor that hard.

When the Cherub was finally out of sight and out of earshot, Maux decided it was time to lighten their mood, and approached with chuckles of his own.

"You look like the front of a box of candy hearts!"

Chapter 19

Anteros mouth hung open in disbelief as the Goblin disappeared out of existence before him. *That little shit left us here!?* Ant wasn't broken anymore, he was kind of angry actually. No, scratch that, Anteros was pissed off!

"Well, I'm not waitin around here," said a rocky voice from the back of the room. Ant turned to witness Emet getting up as if nothing had happened, apparently having made a full recovery once he'd fully eaten Maux's biscuit. "Nobody hurts my Sindri and gets away with it!" Emet cried out as he swung with all his giant might at the bars enclosing them. At first nothing happened, but then he swung again, and again, and another, and another, and slowly the bar's integrity began to fail and with a decent pull the stone man was able to wrench the bars free, giving his party a makeshift exit.

Anteros was impressed by the feat of strength, as he watched Emet turn around and embrace Sindri warmly, "My precious," the stone man whispered in her ear.

Nereid hefted Ant's diaper bag, and the four of them escaped out into the hallway as a claxon sounded around them, and like clockwork a Cyclops rounded the corner with a shocked expression on his face.

No one even had time to utter a word as Emet leapt towards their adversary and nailed him hard with a rocky punch.

Straight in the dick.

Even Anteros had to balk at the hit as the Cyclops crumpled to the ground, and Emet proceeded to nail him in the eyeball, knocking him out. Emet let out a "Whoop!" as yet another figure rounded the hallway after him.

This one a small, floating baby, with green aura trailing behind him. "How the hades did you…?" Ant's father exclaimed before Anteros reached down to his thigh and grabbed…nothing. There was nothing but exposed skin, he had on only a diaper at this point and lacked any weaponry to speak of.

"Looks like I, uh, caught you wit your pants down, eh boyo?" the Cherub said with a wry grin. At a snap of his fingers the other members of his party froze in place, Anteros struggling to come up with a correct move.

"I guess we'll settle this now, show me what you got kid," the Cherub raised his tiny arms and egged him on, "come on!"

There was only one answer. Ant might not be a full fledged Cherub, he might not be anything but a half-breed demigod, but he had access to primordial magic the same as any Olympiad. Normally, he'd channel such raw force through an object, such as his arrows. Anteros wasn't like Maux, he wasn't a wizard, he didn't arrive at his spells via study and practice. It was more natural for him, but also more dangerous.

Ant gathered up all the muster he could, concentrating his energy on his palms, bringing them together at his side, were it not for him being dressed in merely an adult diaper, he might've looked like a character straight out of *Street Fighter* or *Dragonball Z* as a ball of energy began to form between his hands and he concentrated, difficult as it was with the crackling pops and strikes threatening to envelope his person whole, drawing in the powers of Mount Olympus as he directed this energy outward and fired! A long beam of white-blue light extending out from his fingertips and into the outstretched arm of the Cherub.

"This all ya got?" his father yawned as he continued to channel Anteros' stream of energy. "Surely you can do better than dis?" the Cherub continued to taunt him. In his peripheral vision he saw Sindri and Emet frozen in place, and on his other flank stood Nereid with her eyes full of worry at Ant even attempting to channel raw magic. He couldn't let them down, they were counting on him. For all he knew, the multiverse itself was counting on him!

"AAAAAARRRRGGGGHHH!!!!!" the scream was every bit as primal out of Anteros as the magic he was streaming as the beam grew larger and larger, Ant could feel tendons releasing and his own mind was slipping into the void. That was the problem with raw magic, like the portals utilized by the Ferryman, it connected to every possible world, and mortal minds weren't generally capable of perceiving such an expanse safely, and Anteros peering into not just worlds he'd been to like Azurefel Forest, and Olgolgarium, but every single possible world threatened to envelop his mind like so much white noise.

But he was not enveloped. Whether it was residual from his brief time as a Cherub or growth in his abilities as a part of everything he'd been through so far, Anteros survived, and thrived! Slowly the Cherub's calm was broken as he was forced by the weight of the magic to push out a green beam of his own to counter. The two sat at a stalemate for a few moments until it took so much that Ant's father's attention was fully devoted to dueling Anteros, rather than maintaining his spell and his friends broke free!

Sindri grabbed the club from the now prone and knocked out Cyclops and swung it like a golf club into the face of Ant's father, smashing him into the side of the prison wall and knocking him out. The energy he'd been forced to expel taking so much out of the Cherub that it was enough to take him down cold. A smell told Ant that his father had also pooped his swaddling via the effort as well. Anteros threw his head back in laughter, not even caring that his own diaper was wet itself at this point.

"What's so funny?" Nereid asked, confused. "I can finally laugh about somebody else shitting themselves for a change," Ant replied with a grin. The four of them had a decent laugh about that before a new sound touched Ant's inner ear.

"*<As funny as this may be, Mortals, I'd appreciate it if we got a move on>,*" the sound was in Ancient Olympian. A chorus of ancient greek voices from a single mouth that must have sounded very alien to the Dwarf and Giant listening in.

"*<My father is being kept prisoner of his own realm, you must free me!>*"

Anteros and Nereid walked around to another jail cell, this one seeming to get larger and larger as they approached. Reality distortion. *Must be a God in here*, Ant thought. And when the figure inside came into full view it became readily apparent exactly who was entrapped in this particular jail cell. She held a classical Corinthian helm, and was dressed in a long flowing white gown.

It was Minerva herself.

Anteros instinctively kneeled before her. "Hey, what gives?" Emet yelled from around the corner, "Yeah, what's goin on?" came the accompanying squeak. "QUIET!" Nereid yelled back, in her most motherly commanding tone yet.

"*<The Cherub betrayed us, he wanted a "big boy" job. Ha! Juno and Neptune locked me in here, and decided to throw him my job as a bone. Guess nobody wanted it. Justice is a profitless toil!>*"

At this point Nereid was translating for their friends, while Anteros went to grab the keys from the Centurion armor of the Cyclops guard. As he approached the cell, however, not only did the keys distort to an incredibly large size, but they of their own volition floated up and into the awaiting hand of Minerva.

"*<The Cherub didn't dare come near me with these. Not until you convinced him I'd escaped somehow already>*," Minerva said plainly as she unlocked her own cell and exited, stretching in the quickly distorted hallway.

"*<Come>*" She said as the four of them floated up against their will and found themselves sitting atop Minerva's helm, a front row seat to the events they'd set in motion as a long spear appeared in Minerva's hand, buckler shield in the other.

"*<We take back my father's kingdom>*"

…

Maux felt bad about leaving his friends in that cell as he ran his way down the jewel encrusted boulevard, but honestly he figured they'd probably be safer there. His mission now needed stealth, not a bunch of armor-clad adventurers busting up the place.

No, his diapered goblin butt was all that was necessary for this next move. Using the map he'd obtained from the Library made the palace fairly easy to find, and with all of the Cyclopes and Hoplites recently stationed nearer the pearly gates, he found his path relatively unimpeded as he finally neared the end of the jeweled boulevard terminating at the foot of the most massive golden columned building in all of Mount Olympus.

This time the jewels didn't stop at the building either, it was as if the roads were designed to seem as though they spread out from the palace itself, crawling up the columns and onto the roof. It looked like the building was made of the roads spiraling out from it. It was truly an impressive sight to behold, unlike anything Maux had ever come across in his life.

But that was when he hit his first snag as all of a sudden his diaper was visible to him. His hoodie plainly read "Hugs" in red letters for all to see. He was no longer invisible.

The palace must have some sort of magical dampening of some kind Maux figured. He'd have to rely on his Goblinoid stealth from this point forward. He gulped as he felt the warmth spreading in his diaper area.

Maux attempted to skirt around one of the columns when he saw a massive winged horse sitting out front, his wings chained to the ground. He looked miserable, like he'd been stuck this way for some time.

The Goblin felt for him pretty hard, he was clearly Hercules horse, the Pegasus. No surprise that Juno would take out vengeance upon Jupiter's illegitimate son, but having done so well in the past, Maux struggled to figure out the point of hurting the horse at this point. He didn't have anything to do with it. *Gods*, he thought as he decided he would help the creature.

He might not have magic, but the chains were still metal, and he still had a few Goblinoid tricks up his sleeve. Removing some components from his spell pouch, he combined them into a powerful acid and placed some drops on the large chainlinks surrounding the mighty steed, instantly seeing results as it began to eat through them and weaken their bonds.

Pegasus let out a loud NEIGH! as he stretched his wings, broken chains falling to the ground and took off, flying into the sky, circling the palace overhead. Maux smiled, he was happy to do a good deed when he could.

Maux strode as quietly as he could into the doorway just as a couple dozen Hoplites came pouring out of it, clearly drawn by the noise of Pegasus and gave chase to him. Maux grinned, they didn't even notice the Goblin sneaking past them within.

The palace chamber was truly massive, reality distortion in full effect from the many Gods and Goddesses currently in attendance and holding court before a dual throne atop which sat Neptune and Juno, being fed grapes and cheeses by courtesans in kind. Behind them was a bit of a shocking sight, as bound in rawhide and completely immobile on a platform behind the dual throne was the king of the Gods himself, Jupiter.

There were other Gods in attendance, Maux recognized Mars, a distant relative of Anteros, Triton, accompanied by several Daimones apparently feeding him in place of courtesans. Apollo, Venus, and many others. *I wonder what the old man did to piss them all off?* Maux thought. What he did to Juno? Well that was basically common knowledge to everyone, and Neptune had always been a bit jealous of his brother from his underwater domain. But the others? Maux couldn't wrap his mind around a lust for power that strong.

"*<Why don't we strike NOW!?>*" yelled out Neptune in Ancient Olympian. His thunderous voice punctuated by his shaking seaweed hair and slamming his barnacle encrusted fist down upon the arm of the throne.

"*<Be patient, brother>*," Juno replied in a much more calm manner. A calm and cold demeanor that sent chills down Maux's spine, no stranger to chills himself. "*<The Humans must flood the Earth themselves, or else their faith will not be genuine. Remember your failure at the Acropolis>*," Juno continued, and even Maux could tell that was a deep jab. Long ago Neptune had competed with Minerva for control over the city of Athens, and Neptune attempted to force the issue by striking the ground with his Trident, causing a spring to gush forth, or so the legend goes. But the spring was salty and unable to provide any particularly useful benefit to the people, who instead turned their attentions to Minerva whom had provided them with the incredibly useful Olive tree. The town was named in her honor by their name for the Goddess, Athena.

The argument was the perfect cover for him to sneak around. Entering the middle of the throne room, Maux crept beneath the large table on which the fruits and other such treats were being handed out amongst the Gods.

The reality distortion made Maux feel like he was in *Alice in Wonderland* or *The Wizard of Oz* or something as the table felt like a skyscraper with this many deities in attendance. It took him forever to reach its end, and there was much avoidance of toes and feet, whom kept reaching out to kick him with gusts as their sandaled limbs switched positions.

But reach its end he finally did, and he slipped just out of sight of the two Gods on the thrones. He saw the marble platform raised behind them and the eyeball of Jupiter stare directly into Maux's own. It looked like it contained the multiverse itself within his iris, streaked with lightning. His beard and massive mane of hair were as black as the night sky, and he was completely naked beneath his rawhide entrapments.

Maux climbed atop the platform and waddled his way towards Jupiter's ear. "I apologize for my rudeness, Sire, but I'm gonna try and rescue you!" and Maux could've sworn he'd saw the God give a nearly imperceptible smirk and definitely gave the Goblin a wink which took Maux completely by surprise. All of a sudden he couldn't see his diaper on him, and he'd gone completely invisible once again.

Of course Jupiter can control his own throne room! Maux thought, as he grinned in kind. And Maux proceeded to whisper a spell that created four more clones of himself that went to work scrambling all over the God. They weren't true clones, merely illusions that could interact with the environment, and they lacked independent thought, merely repeating a mindless task Maux concentrated on. In this case, freeing the King of the Gods.

Neptune and Juno's plan was simple, straight out of *The Iliad* as Jupiter was tied down in rawhide, with hundreds of tiny knots. Gambling that the strength would be enough to hold the old man down, and that the size he had obtained in his throne room would prevent him from ever undoing any of the tiny knots in the chord.

They covered their tracks, there would be no Briareos in this version of the story. But what they hadn't counted on was mortals defending their own realm, nor had they counted upon the dexterity and ingenuity of a Goblin being the one to be their undoing.

The knots were so tiny that they were actually perfect size to be undone by Maux himself, though this meant that they were so numerous that the Goblin was quickly beginning to tire. He couldn't give up though, not when so much was a stake. Maux pressed onward, untying and untying as fast as he could, his magical clones repeating his actions dozens of times over.

Just as the argument was starting to heat up as to whether Neptune should be allowed to implement a first strike, and just as Maux was starting to think his task just might be impossible, a long golden spear impaled itself in the wall above the platform.

Juno and Neptune looked up in horror and Maux was afraid for a moment that he was fucked, but they were too shocked to even notice a little thing like himself as they leapt to their feet. "*<That fucking baby!>*" Juno exclaimed, and it was everything Maux could do to keep himself from laughing. Cursing just didn't sound right coming from the mouth of the Goddess of the home and the hearth. "*<I told you we shouldn't have entrusted her to the Cherub. He can't even control his bowels!>*" Neptune called out. "*<I didn't hear you complaining about it before you old bag of seaweed!>*" Juno shot back, and Maux caught sight of one of the most powerful images he'd ever seen.

Minerva, wrapped in her most elegant gown, Corinthian Helmet upon her head, came sprinting into the chamber, Gladius held high as Mars jumped to meet her in combat. The God of War was more properly termed the God of Bloodlust, and as talented and accomplished as he was on the field of battle, he was no match for the Goddess of Strategy and Tactics as she cut him down.

Maux then had to go back to the task at hand as he was finally starting to wear down the knots holding the God of the Heavens, Jupiter though, once the binds were weakened enough, took matters into his own hands, and burst forth sending Maux flying off in the opposite direction. The Goblin took advantage of his returning ability to do magic by casting the same feather spell, allowing him and his clones to float gently to the ground, none the worse for wear.

"*<THUNDERBOOOOOOLT!!!>*" Jupiter cried out, and as if on cue a massive stylized bolt of lightning appeared in his hand, and he struck at Neptune with it who fell to his knees and began to beg for mercy. Minerva produced a set of Golden Shackles with which she placed upon Juno's outstretched wrists, as she too fell to her knees in total submission.

Upon restraining of Juno, Minerva kneeled before her father, providing opportunity for Sindri, Emet, Nereid, and Anteros to hop off her helmet and greet four copies of their Goblinoid friend once he'd lowered his hoodie and broken the spell. "You found Minerva!?" "You found Jupiter!?" their respective parties both exclaimed at the same time as Maux's clones poofed out of existence, before bursting into fits of laughter.

Chapter 20

The feast was legendary, and their party was resplendent in the finest garments they'd ever worn at the behest of Jupiter himself. Sindri was in a fashionable traditional Dwarven tunic and pants, but in different shades of pastel pink, Emet had on a fine white formal shirt and black pants, Maux in a powder blue tuxedo onesie, and the finest of them all to Ant's eyes, Nereid was in a bright gold sequined gown and matching heels.

Arm in arm with Anteros in a fine tuxedo the five strode into the Palace ballroom, a magical floating chandelier shining brightly as the various foods and wines and beers were flowing throughout. Neptune had been banished to the depths of the oceans, and Juno was hung from the sky in punishment, but those that had remained loyal to Jupiter were all in attendance, including, of course Minerva, the Ferryman, Diana, Bacchus, and a host of other minor gods and goddesses. Even Hades made an extremely rare appearance, glaring from beneath his helmet at the frivolities before him. The closest thing to emotion the ruler of the underworld ever truly showed, despite Persephone's ardent attempts to cheer him up, itself a rare occurrence as on Mount Olympus she could be with him in the summertime, much to her mother's chagrin.

"Ah yes, the heroes of the hour!" Jupiter said warmly from his throne at the head of the magnificent feasting area, now singular in the middle. He dropped his usual Ancient Olympian in honor of his guests. Anteros was a bit uncomfortable in his tuxedo, however. Everyone else seemed to be in their most enjoyable gear, but his seemed a bit random, he'd only ever worn a tuxedo once. Jupiter gave a quizzical look and Anteros got the distinct impression their clothes were chosen from their happiest memories, and Ant and Nereid's were chosen from their experience at the Belle Côte, and while that was a safe bet for his happiest memory, his clothing wasn't something he'd been comfortable with at the time.

Jupiter could peer into the souls of men and all of a sudden Anteros was standing, clad in a Power Rangers t-shirt and Diaper. His first instinct was to be embarrassed, but Ant was no longer the same guy he was at the beginning of this adventure. Anteros had gotten friendship, companionship, and a renewed confidence in who he was.

Ant smiled, and Nereid smirked as in her hand a pacifier formed out of thin air as she pulled him in, kissed him hard, and she shoved the paci in his mouth. Anteros was finally happy and comfortable in his surroundings as the two of them danced to the soft music of the Muses, next to a happily embraced Sindri and Emet.

"One in particular of your number must be recognized for singular efforts towards yours truly," Jupiter proclaimed, rising from his throne. "You, little one, arise and be counted!" the God called out. Maux had been tapping his foot slowly to the song and was shocked to find a spotlight had magically appeared above his person.

"Uh, yeah...sire?" Maux spoke up with some trepidation as all eyes in the room trained upon him and the Muses fell to silence.

"What is it you truly desire? A reward for freeing me, personally," Jupiter boomed. Maux thought for a moment, his first thought was for him to have been born a normal Goblin, a thing he'd wished for his entire life, but as he looked at Anteros, Nereid, Sindri, and Emet and down at his own tuxedo onesie, he realized that his being different was what allowed all of this to happen in the first place, and he couldn't let that go now. He just wished there wasn't such terrible consequences for it.

"It shall be done," Jupiter proclaimed, and Maux's face turned to extreme horror, "Wait, no! I didn't....!" but the Goblin's pleas fell upon deaf ears as Jupiter nodded to the right of the room.

"Hades, brother, if you could do the honors," Jupiter said the request with a smile as Hades arose, helm of invisibility held aloft as he placed it upon his head, the only thing visible of his person now being the bright icy blue piercing gaze of the one who controls the veil.

From the entrance of the great hall stepped a slightly larger, muscular Goblin dressed in a rag tunic and carrying a spear. His eyes were solid red, like Maux's and though his face wore an expression of shock and awe at his newfound surroundings, one could tell his mouth was filled with rows of tiny sharp teeth. He looked about ready to bolt until he locked eyes with Maux.

Maux beamed, his shock and awe turning to tears as he ran as fast as he could waddling with a diaper and embraced the new arrival, "PAPA!!" and Maux's father dropped the spear and returned the embrace hard.

For once, everything was right in the world.

Epilogue

Nereid was humming the soft tune of the Muses as the images of diapered Anteros and herself in her shimmering gold gown dancing on Jupiter's ballroom floor replayed themselves in her mind as she walked up the steps in front of Ant's apartment in Starkville. She was carrying a couple of bags of groceries, having picked them up on the way home from class.

It was fall semester now, and Nereid had also enrolled in Mississippi State, attempting to advance higher than her lowly secretarial role at Glaucus' Trident Industries. Glaucus never received punishment, as he was able to parlay both his lack of notoriety, as well as his general slimy personality into a 'Get out of Jail Free' card of sorts, though he and Nereid were no longer on speaking terms. Juno was eventually released from her heavenly prison after her cries of pain became unbearable for the other deities, on the condition that she never attempted something like that ever again.

"How're my boys?" Nereid asked brightly as she opened the door to the apartment to find Anteros and Maux gaming away on their computers. "Fine," the two of them said in unison, as Ant arose, pulling up his diaper as he did so, and reached out to kiss her, and Nereid laughed as she returned it but nearly dropped her groceries as a result. "Hold on, hold on," Nereid she said with a smile, "you're gonna make me drop them."

"Sorry boo boo, I just missed you," Ant replied. "We were just doing some raids with Sindri and Emet," Maux piped in from his desk, also in t-shirt and diaper, teething ring drooping slightly in his mouth, "Wanna hop on?"

"Maybe in a minute," Nereid replied as she inspected Ant's diaper area, "I think somebody here needs a change," all of the little paws on the front had disappeared.

"It's me, isn't it?" Anteros said with mock embarrassment. "Yes, it's you, ya butt," Nereid replied with a chuckle.

Just another day in paradise...

Milton Keynes UK
Ingram Content Group UK Ltd.
UKHW020742150324
439439UK00013B/1323